Falling *in* Love While Stuffing *a* Zebra

Falling *in* Love While Stuffing *a* Zebra

A Philosophical Tale

ROLAND KUPERS

GREENLEAF
BOOK GROUP PRESS

This is a work of fiction. Although most of the characters, organizations, and events portrayed in the novel are based on actual historical counterparts, the dialogue and thoughts of these characters are products of the author's imagination.

Published by Greenleaf Book Group Press
Austin, Texas
www.gbgpress.com

Distributed by Greenleaf Book Group

For ordering information or special discounts for bulk purchases, please contact Greenleaf Book Group at PO Box 91869, Austin, TX 78709, 512.891.6100.

Design and composition by Greenleaf Book Group and Mimi Bark
Cover design by Greenleaf Book Group and Mimi Bark
Cover images used under license from © Marvin Nast

Publisher's Cataloging-in-Publication data is available.

Print ISBN: 979-8-88645-356-0

eBook ISBN: 979-8-88645-357-7

To offset the number of trees consumed in the printing of our books, Greenleaf donates a portion of the proceeds from each printing to the Arbor Day Foundation. Greenleaf Book Group has replaced over 50,000 trees since 2007.

Printed in the United States of America on acid-free paper

25 26 27 28 29 30 31 10 9 8 7 6 5 4 3 2 1

First Edition

To my father's love of the bon mot,
Hester's limitless enthusiasm,
Rebecca's whimsical determination,
and Madame de Staël, the Marquis de Condorcet,
and Benjamin Franklin—
bien étonnés de se trouver ensemble.[1]
They all helped brew this tale of complexity.

1 The French expression "bien étonnés de se trouver ensemble" is used to denote a situation in which unlikely companions, much to their own surprise, find themselves having the same intentions, goals, or interests.

Contents

1

A Wild Ass

Paris, Saturday, November 11, 1786

Startled by the sound of the small cannon firing its blank charge, George du Paon awoke. He realised that noon had passed, as that is when the miniature cannon announced mid-day in the gardens of the Palais-Royal. A few uncomfortable and interrupted hours of sleep slumped on a wooden bench had made his back sore. His limbs had stiffened in the cool air; after a night of debate and debauchery, an indulgent slumber had slipped into a late Saturday-morning nap. The gardens were now pleasantly quiet after the bustling rowdiness of the evening and night. George briefly basked in the silence—only interrupted by the sound of brooms sweeping the gravel avenues under the trees.

It was past time to get to work.

The autumn colours were all around, offsetting the pale rows of columns along each side of the vast rectangular courtyard of the Palais-Royal gardens.

Closely hugging the buildings protruding from the palace itself, each of the round grooved columns was coifed with a sober Doric capital. Above them, exuberant columns with Corinthian capitals embraced the gardens, bushels of acanthus leaves topping the arcades and rows of vases lining their summit.

The lime trees in the garden grasped their remaining leaves, straight-jacketed into neat lines by an invisible army of ladder-climbing gardeners. Their rigorous geometry formed a quiet reproach to the baroque ornamentation above thc bay windows along the façades.

When he had first visited the gardens after their reopening in '84, George had been struck by the determined effort to encapsulate nature in neat lines and ornaments. He now relished the irony that it had become the place where both ideas and desires most freely flowed. The little cannon had been a great addition. A lens amplifying the sun's rays lighted the gunpowder, albeit with the unfortunate side effect that it had to be fired manually on overcast days.

Subsequently, another one of the habituals, Jacques Delille, famous for his bon mots, had written a short poem on the ardours and arbours of the Palais-Royal: "In this garden one encounters neither fields nor meadows, nor woods, nor flowers. And, even if habits are upended there, at least one's watch may be set."[1] George recalled a wine-imbibed evening when he had unusually wandered beyond his habitual cafés in the Palais-Royal and had met Delille, as they found themselves at the same table. They had explored at length the importance of

1 "Dans ce jardin on ne rencontre. Ni champs, ni prés, ni bois, ni fleurs. Et si l'on y dérègle ses mœurs, Au moins on y règle sa montre." Source: Delille, "Dans ce jardin on ne rencontre."

knowing time precisely, albeit with a granularity only sensible with mild intoxication.

A keen sailor, Delille had recalled the great invention of the Yorkshire working-class master-clockmaker John Harrison, who had solved the mighty longitude problem for ship navigation only seventeen years prior. However, the grand allocated prize and the recognition promised by the Royal Society had been withheld from him, largely because Harrison did not fit the mould of the British scientist. Somewhat randomly, George and Delille had rejoiced that at least in France, precise time was available to all through a daily cannon shot.

Now, with an uneasy gait, George headed towards the northern exit of the garden, past the theatre where the actors were filing in to practice for the evening's performance. He observed that most were clad in the well-worn rough linen clothing that identified those with high hopes but limited means. One man stood out in an ill-fitting bright blue silk coat with white ribbons, hinting at an affair with a wealthy admirer who had left the frock as a reward. The two women behind him had likely found the same route to better clothes, but at least they had had the coquetry to make their gifted dresses fit tightly. Actresses and actors were in great demand in the Palais-Royal, both for their good looks and for their ability to shift between identities to the whim of their admirers after the evening applause had dimmed.

Crossing into the gardens of the Tuileries Palace, he felt his head clearing and his senses sharpening.[2] Their wide expanses

---

2 In 1667, at the request of the famous author of *Sleeping Beauty* and other fairy tales, Charles Perrault, the Tuileries Garden was opened to the public, with the exception of beggars,

onto the Seine on the south side contrasted with the restricted space of the Palais-Royal. The relative anonymity of those who strolled the gardens was a relief from the social, intellectual, and sensual intensity of his evening's redoubt.

In these gardens, the trees were less controlled. The moss accumulating on the soaring statues celebrating the fame of Louis XIV amplified this sense of laissez-faire. The jumble of colours painted on the autumn leaves echoed the absence of willed aesthetics.

When George finally crossed the moat's turning bridge and emerged onto la place Louis XV, he was ready to plunge into his workday.[3] In the middle of the square stood a somewhat pompous equestrian statue of Louis XV—which Jefferson would express his disapproval of and warn Congress against considering a similar tribute to George Washington. The long, ornate, columned façade along the north side of the square, framing the space between the jumbled trees of the Tuileries gardens and the martial grounds of the Champs-Élysées, had been designed a decade and a half earlier by Gabriel. It was one of the first urban commissions in Paris—which hitherto had been mostly limited to religious edifices.

George was stopped from crossing the street by a long parade of horse-drawn wagons covered in black tarps. Ahead of

---

"lackeys," and soldiers. It was the first royal garden to be open to the public. Source: "Tuileries Garden," Wikipedia.

3 A movable bridge, a *pont-tournant*, was placed at the west end over the moat to make access to the garden easier. The creation of la place Louis XV (now place de la Concorde) created a grand vestibule to the garden.

the procession were men carrying torches, and between them priests chanting the Mass of the Dead. The Parisian cemeteries were overflowing with corpses. The living were clamouring for more space; the dead needed to move away, driven by their inexorable growth in numbers, as generation succeeded generation. A solution was found. The chain of wagons was transferring six million skeletons into the vast labyrinths carved over centuries in the limestone beneath the city. On a prior year's visit to these catacombs, as he walked through the tunnels carved under Paris, George had witnessed the bones sorted and stacked, femur upon femur, skull upon skull, and so on. It had struck him that his work was always concerned with the external shape of animals and that he never dealt in bones, which were a mere afterthought, and yet through their presence, millions of people retained a small toehold in today's reality. At the thought of his sister's bones, tears briefly surged to his eyes, as if propelled by a great pressure. Violette would have laughed dismissively at the mere thought of her bones being separated, sorted, and stacked.

Crossing the Seine, now walking at a brisk pace, he soon reached his atelier in the rue des Saints-Pères. The large oak doors onto the street were open, as was usual during the day. At the back of the second courtyard, he was engulfed by the familiar, mildly nauseating smell of formaldehyde from the atelier.

The workshop was the reign of his collaborators Gaston and Jeanne. They greeted him gaily, displaying not the slightest surprise at his late arrival. They were used to the alternative daily rhythm that distinguished the social strata.

When Gaston had started his employment over a decade before, he'd been very slim, but over the years, he'd grown both in size and in confidence. His girth, gradually expanding over the period, testified to the ample food that the workers enjoyed. Gaston interrupted his whistling to greet his employer with a joyous "Monsieur! You've returned. I hope your lunch was as good as ours. Jeanne only barely touched hers, so I enjoyed it for the both of us." His dark hair and eyes were offset by an even and joyous nature.

George had learnt to value Gaston's loyalty over his wits. Whenever Gaston left the atelier for his weekly visit to his brother in Saint Denis, his whistling echoed in the street, bouncing between the façades. He never failed to return with a bottle from his brother's meagre wine trade, which notwithstanding its basic nature, he insisted on sharing with Jeanne and George.

Jeanne pushed Gaston aside. "Monsieur George, you must see what has just been delivered!"

At twenty-one, Jeanne's steadfastness exuded seriousness, the sparkle in her eyes cast a mineral hardness that betrayed the harshness of her early years. Her lips had acquired the slightest Parisian pout. Her head tilted upwards, making her carved nose more enticing and prominent, and her chestnut hair flowed down the back to the hem of her corset.

George observed how she complemented Gaston's rougher presence with the undulating movements of her hands. But years of scrubbing floors and later carcasses had left a coarse imprint on those hands.

A client appeared in the entrance, and Jeanne smiled and bowed slightly. “I am sorry, sir,” she politely told the man, “we are closed today, but if you can come back tomorrow, I will be very happy to show you all the new work.”

The man smiled back and made his retreat.

Jeanne’s unmistakable charm had become an additional enticement for George’s clients to remain faithful to the atelier. Du Paon’s firm was much sought after and his business was thriving, but most commissions consisted of mere foxes, deer, rabbits, or the odd peacock.

Jeanne closed the door and walked to the back of the room towards the new arrival.

“Well done,” said George, in appreciation of Jeanne’s elegant handling of the client. “With such a charming rejection, he may well return.”

The highlight of the morning had been a poorly cleaned new delivery betraying a disarming lack of skill. Jeanne had laid out the animal on the large wooden table at the centre of the back room of the workshop so they could all observe the sample.

After the initial thrill at the sight of the striped beast, George observed the deficiencies in its preparation and frowned. “This is very messy. Who prepared this? Where on earth did they learn their trade? I do hope that we can repair this.”

Jeanne looked deeply concerned, then suddenly delighted. “These stripes! Not at all like a cow, much as if it was painted by someone. And so big!”

Salt had conserved the inside merely adequately, but George was relieved to see that the outer skin had remained in perfect condition. This would be critical in obtaining the high-level result that the queen would surely expect.

"How should we proceed?" asked Jeanne as she bit her lip.

Such an exotic animal was the rarest of challenges. Alive, along with its sibling, it had been a present given in 1762 to the young Queen of England, a welcome distraction a year after her marriage to the rather dull King George III.

Before considering how to proceed, George stared at the striped apparition, recalling how it had been mentioned many times in the *Journal de Paris*. "Let me describe its English background a little. You realise the remarkable item we have here, right?"

"I always thought the English were strange, and their animals as well," ventured Gaston.

"No, no really, these animals do not live in England," George reassured him. "It comes from the south of the African continent. This one survived the long journey from the Cape of Good Hope, alongside its sibling, to England, where it was offered to the queen—and then went on to live to a remarkably old age—that alone should impress us. The queen had grown so excessively fond of it that she wanted it eternalised. That is how it has made its way to Paris."

The zebra had been a source of inspiration for the satirist's pens of the day, and George recalled one particularly bawdy song which he recited to his collaborators:

"Though squeamish old Prudes with Invective and Spleen,
May turn up their Noses and censure the Queen;
Crying out, 'Tis a Shame, that her Queenship, alas

Should take such a Pride—in exposing her Ass.'"

"Ass!" screamed Gaston in delight.

A text from the English court had been delivered along with the skin, and it related the story of the animal. George loosely quoted from it: "While the first zebra had been given away and finished stuffed in the Blue Boar pub in York, in keeping with the fashion to exhibit exotic animals in taverns and coffee houses, the queen, it seemed, desired a more deserving afterlife for her second one. The first one had been rapidly decaying through the ineptitude of an insufficiently skilled taxidermist. The Leverian collection at Leicester House was a great favourite of the queen. She had ordered the collection to be open and at no cost for visitors, a generous gesture her court had sought to temper by making the free access contingent on arriving in a private carriage."

Skipping past a few less interesting paragraphs, George went on. "As the queen intended the second zebra to be included in the Leverian, she apparently sought out the most reputable artisans in Europe to conserve the animal. This led to the crate with the zebra materialising on this November day in the rue des Saints-Pères, on our doorstep. The choice of a French master over a British one was made barely palatable by a brief lull in the habitual tensions between our countries."

A bundle of prints and a folder with several dozen drawings had been delivered along with the skin. George peered over Jeanne's shoulder as she sifted through them. "It appears that an added benefit of the sordid past of the widely mocked 'Queen's Asses,'" George said, "is that there is no shortage of sketches and drawings of the animals during their lives." Since neither George nor any of his collaborators had ever seen a zebra, these images were of essential importance to their work.

"Last year they painted a horse for carnival. I thought it was a bad joke, but this one seems to have been created with stripes!" blurted out Gaston.

"They do look like grazing donkeys on the drawings," Jeanne added, setting the stack of drawings down on a nearby cabinet, "but somehow more muscular, more ready to pounce."

There was an additional reason why this commission was so important to George, and he was keen to discuss the history of the beast with his friend Nicolas de Condorcet during his next visit to the Palais-Royal. Well-read and well-connected, he would no doubt have an original view. Nicolas was a most prominent economist, mathematician, and nobleman. Their friendship was an improbable one—which made George all the more grateful for it. Sharing a compulsion to observe the world from a distance, Nicolas and George had become close friends, notwithstanding the gap in their social rank. They met regularly, most often at one of the cafés in the Palais-Royal, and thrived through each other's observations and speculations on the challenges of the times.

A regular at court, Nicolas had told him of the zebra that lived at the Versailles court and was the subject of many experiments. "Buffon," Nicolas explained, on one of their recent outings, "wanted to understand whether they might improve the species, perhaps by crossing it with a French female ass."

The main court naturalist Louis Leclerc Comte de Buffon was a shared acquaintance.

"Buffon has been a great supporter of my workshop, and I owe him much gratitude. You, my friend, probably owe him much champagne!" George had commented in jest.

With a brief smile, Nicolas had gone on to describe the outcome of Buffon's efforts. "Alas," he told George, a sparkle in his eye, "the zebra spurned all attempts at forced courtship. Painting stripes on the unfortunate French ass could equally not excite the Versailles zebra. The comte had concluded that this coldness could not be attributed to another cause than the disagreement of their natures, for this zebra was then four years of age and was very lively in every other exercise."

George had heard from a colleague naturalist that this experiment was widely followed with considerable interest, as zebras were notoriously untameable, contrary to their European cousins, who were the very metaphor of domestic servitude in the city, farm, and on the battlefield. The inability of man to subjugate the zebra, a beast so much a horse in its likeness, was felt as a notable failure.

This had an impact well beyond the loss of an ornamental carriage puller, casting a shadow over the essence of the relationship of man with the natural world. Although eroding under the rise of the scientific mind, George regularly observed how the biblical realm still strongly shaped expectations. He had heard directly, alongside many of his colleagues, how perfectly legitimate scientific explanations grounded in empirical observations struggled to displace revealed knowledge from scripture. The dominion of man over nature trumpeted by Genesis 1:26 went mostly unchallenged.

George mumbled to Jeanne almost inaudibly, "'And God said, let us make man in our image, after our likeness: and let them have dominion over the fish of the sea, and over the fowl of the air, and over the cattle, and over all the earth, and over every creeping thing that creepeth upon the earth.'"

"What?" said Jeanne, and George resisted the urge to smile—clearly she was unaccustomed to hearing her master quote scripture. "I don't recall this in last week's mass," she added mischievously. "If my memory serves me correctly, I recall you had slept late, and I had gone ahead with Gaston."

"My apologies, Jeanne and Gaston, I was then and am now quite exhausted and will retire. I'll be back down in a few hours." George acutely felt the aches from his morning on the park bench.

"Here are some sketches I have made for the zebra," Jeanne called out in mild rebuke. From a wide drawer under the table, she pulled out a big sheet of paper that showed various equine positions. George noticed that they bore a distant resemblance to the statues that had served as backdrop during Jeanne's education in her previous workshop.

George replied in a flat tone, betraying his lack of sleep, "Thank you, Jeanne. I see you've been diligently studying horses, as we had discussed."

"Indeed, she has," interjected Gaston. "She has even got me to stop a carriage in the street. She wanted to see what the muscles looked like when the horses get back into motion. The owners did not look happy, not happy they were."

The atelier's aim in the preparation of the animal would be to represent this tension, how the zebra had defied the best efforts of the court's scientists at imposing man's will on the natural world. George's zebra would incarnate the vitality of nature.

Jeanne looked at George with despair. "Do you not like the drawings? Perhaps you're right. I should have drawn more different kinds of horses, perhaps the funny Flemish ones with the broad legs and big buttocks."

His lack of reaction to the drawings clearly worried her. George knew about her lack of confidence and noticed it now, but his tiredness hardened him into being less considerate than usual.

Her previous employer's recommendation contradicted her self-image, as he had praised her highly. Robert-Guillaume Dardel was an acquaintance of George, a member of an informal league of ateliers that were highly regarded by their wealthy clients, and they regularly provided recommendations for work to each other. Dardel's workshop had become fashionable as a source of portraits and busts for minor aristocrats and newly wealthy members of the bourgeoisie.

A year earlier, he had come to George to place Jeanne—one of his collaborators. "She was orphaned at an early age and was fortunate enough to be hired by my atelier to clean and order the halls," Dardel had said, although with fondness. "Many evenings before retiring to her room in the servant's quarters in the small, all-too-well-ventilated rooms under the roof, she lingered in the workshop, doodling sketches in the margins of some discarded papers. When I came in one morning, I was surprised that Jeanne was not there yet. I noticed some drawings that had been left behind on the table in a rush. I had never seen these before and was struck by the assertiveness of the lines, by the sensitivity of the treatment of the shadows. Clearly not the hand of a learned artist, it was nevertheless a gifted one, bearing promise. I queried my apprentices as to whether they were the authors and was met with rebuttals and a grudging acknowledgement of the talent of the draftsman. At no time did I suspect that the unassuming, simple girl who kept order might have been the author."

George had nodded with understanding and had theatrically spread his arms, as if announcing a surprise guest.

Dardel had gone on to explain. "One morning, a complaint from the Marquis Louis Georges Érasme de Contades for the late delivery of a statue for the gardens of his hotel in the rue d'Anjou had sent me back to the atelier later than usual. Hunched over a table, with a thin piece of charcoal in her hand, her coarse grey linen dress hugging her waist and lower back, was Jeanne, absorbed in her sketching. My voice startled her, and she attempted to whisk away the drawing scraps. I noticed her cheeks flush," he added with the precision of a painter, "offsetting the dark colour of the locks escaping underneath the constraints of her plain cream-coloured bonnet."

The accidental discovery of her talent reoriented the direction of her life's glide path. Because of her lowly origins, with the added burden of her gender, the likelihood of escaping eternal servitude—or worse—was grim. Dardel had told George that he had offered her a position to help with the draughting work of the atelier, and her fate improved markedly. She had moved down from the servant's quarters in the attic, into a modest but comfortable room on one of the lower floors.

George had volunteered that it must have been problematic for the other apprentices of the workshop to have a woman working at their side.

Dardel had replied, "Indeed, but I endeavoured to get Jeanne accepted and gave her drawing lessons when the others were gone, but the situation became increasingly untenable. She convinced no one by pointing to Élisabeth Vigée le Brun, whose portrait of Marie Antoinette from 1783 had led to her admission at the Académie royale de peinture et de sculpture."

"Clearly she was also exploring your library, this simple servant of yours," George had observed.

He had heard how Dardel's staff had opposed Jeanne's promotion. "Vigée le Brun was not a cleaning maid," noted her reluctant colleagues. So Jeanne had to go, and Dardel set about looking for a suitable position. After being turned down by his fellow painters and sculptors, it occurred to him that George du Paon might require an artist with an aptitude for sketching animals, and who could perhaps sculpt the models around which the skins were hung.

The first time they met, Jeanne had described to George how she had begun drawing. "One night," she explained, tucking her chestnut curls behind her ears, "I had fallen asleep over the drawings and woken in the middle of the night in the dark and cold atelier. I was startled by the dark and the staring gaze of the white marble people. It felt as if they had woken up and had moved around the room, but the moment I woke up, they froze in their movements. I rushed upstairs and buried myself under the blankets. I was terrified but also excited at the force awoken by pen and paper. I resolved to draw as often as I could."

Now Jeanne was sketching the queen's zebra in George's workshop. After George had observed her squinting over her drawings, he had offered her his father's eyeglasses. Though they were too big for her, the lenses serendipitously offered the proper amount of correction, and she now wore them proudly, sliding them up her nose whenever they slumped.

Jeanne Laplume straightened from a deep hunch over a set of drawings of the zebra. "What do you think?" she asked George, with the assertiveness that characterised her independence but also betrayed a hint of uncertainty.

He recognised the tone and knew he needed to make her comfortable before engaging in a conversation, let alone criticising her designs. "Strong and clear—I like the powerful stance of the back legs, like a horse prepped for battle."

"Yes," she retorted, settling into her identity as an artist, "but I'm not really sure what a zebra is. Is it a small horse or just the ornate cousin of an ass?"

George proceeded to tell her the story of the unhappy experiments with its brethren at Versailles and how zebras defied the dominance of man over nature promised in the Bible through their stubborn refusal to be tamed.

"Really? It could not be domesticated in any way?" She removed the glasses and stared at George.

"Notwithstanding the efforts of all the scientists of the court, it remained the very symbol of wildness. The king dismissed the scientists and called in the horse trainers of the cavalry, but they also failed. In a desperate final attempt, they turned to the farmers of the royal estates, but they, too, fell short."

"Not tamed." She sighed in admiration, leafing through the stack of zebra drawings in the English folder.

"Yes—and to speak to that, what I want is the shape of a cousin of the horse and the ass, but most importantly an expression of the wildness of nature shining through. The Queen of England should be mildly disturbed by seeing our stuffed zebra—it should remind her of the Dionysian convulsions in the immense Rubens ceilings in the Banqueting House at Whitehall. There are some impressions upstairs of those paintings that I made a few years ago in London."

"I'll take a look at the sketches of wild torrents I made during our stay in the Forêt de Fontainebleau last year—and cross the horse with the tempest."

George was confident that she had glimpsed the ambition of the task, and unable to add anything to further stimulate her considerable imagination, he retired to his private apartments above the workshop. A single flight of a broad staircase with concave low steps led from the courtyard to the entrance of George's living quarters on the first-floor landing.

He stopped outside the tall green double doors that separated the outside world from his apartment. His gaze followed the railing that had held the grasp of so many strangers, the stairs winding upwards to neighbours above. He almost never engaged with the other people in the building. They were, he assumed, uncomfortable with the idea that his hands touched lifeless matter so frequently and suspicious that he had never wed.

The dark green double panelled doors opened onto a small hallway that looked down three door openings in a row, providing an immediate perspective to the other end of the apartment, where a narrow winding staircase led to the diminutive room where his servant slept. He had lived here for the last seven years since moving to Paris. Even when it was cold outside, and perhaps even more so, he felt an imperceptible surge in his chest whenever he entered this space—Violette was gone.

•

Violette and George had been symbiotic as children, and inseparable. George remembered how people would comment on it, always in a doting sort of way. "How precious," an overbearing aunt would exclaim. A teacher would scold them for not working more independently. That sort of thing. Had it not been for the attention others poured on them, George wouldn't have noticed how inextricable they were from one another—his twin had always been second nature to him.

Their ability to finish each other's sentences had waned over time, but they continued to hold hands while walking along the Seine or through the Tuileries, shunning the asymmetry of a mere arm hold. "And I'm not an old lady who needs to be steadied," Violette had once said. George replied by rotating both their hands above their heads and smiled at her. Concerned about excessive dependence, their father had insisted that they attend separate schools, until he noticed that this led to even greater closeness in the evenings. As children, they had few other friendships as he and Violette were so close, and though he could not speak for her, he felt entirely content with only her presence to entertain and stimulate him. It was not something they talked about, but he guessed that she felt the same way.

They grew up in a small town near Metz in eastern France, in the strictly segregated social structure of the day. They befriended peasant children for the purpose of play and merely observed the nobility from a suitable distance.

When George moved to Paris to establish the firm, she had remained behind for less than a year, assisting their mother. She soon followed him to the capital, taking the room next to his in the apartment.

George was devastated when Violette had died three years earlier. They had shared the enterprise. She had been the artist, shaping the animals to perfection, expressing ferocity, docility, meanness, or the restrained violence that characterises much of the natural world. Working together had been a natural continuation of the proximity of their youth. While they differed in many ways, small and large, they always sensed precisely what the other was wrestling with. George understood that this was not unusual between twins, but they had lived and worked together inseparably.

Violette was a happier soul than George, finding in every moment a source of joy, ever so small, the potential for some new improvement, or the goodness of any person who crossed the doorstep of the rue des Saints-Pères. She offered roots to George's wandering thoughts, with an earthiness that was always light.

Inevitably bubbling with an inexhaustible supply of energy, she sometimes overreached, causing a tray of tools to tumble or a vat of chemical substance to spill. Gaston was accustomed to these events and rushed to remediate. When she cut her left hand while cleaning the skin of a marmot, no one gave it a second thought. The wound was quickly cleaned and bound, and she continued to work as best as she could the same afternoon. Over the next days, the arm reddened increasingly, and she became bedridden with a rising fever. George had called for a doctor who had bled her more—which besides being counterintuitive was also counterproductive. The fever kept rising, and she gradually grew more distant. George sat by her bedside from the third day, sensing and fearing the worst. At dawn of the sixth day, her arm swollen, the fever blistering, Violette was dead.

George had thrown himself into his work and was grateful that Jeanne had been recommended to him by Dardel to assist him. But he found himself fleeing more regularly to the earthly pleasures and the intellectual jousts at the Palais-Royal.

This evening, having agreed upon the next steps for the queen's zebra with Jeanne in the atelier and craving quietude, he took the stairs to his flat. Light poured in through five tall double windows along the courtyard to the left of the entrance door. Each window provided a perspective on the courtyard below, through the translucent branches of an acacia tree in its centre. Each room was sparsely, if elegantly, furnished, and dominated by sober marble chimney mantles bearing a small oval portrait under the simply ornamented mirrors.

A dog barked in the distance.

2

George du Paon

At seven, George awoke. He lay still for the briefest moment in the stalled state between sleep and wakefulness when thoughts stray and tumble uncontrolled, the mind still unconstrained by the formalism and habits of consciousness. Trees, zebras, colours, and patterns competed for attention in a synchronised minuet. It had always been the most creative moment of his day, when thoughts and patterns from the previous day, hustled in dreams, suddenly blended.

This morning, no revelations, as the creaking sound of the bedroom door announced his valet Jacques bearing breakfast. George made a mental note to bring back some grease from the workshop to lubricate the door hinges.

Jacques put down the tray with a cup of chocolate, Haitian cane sugar, a large glass of water, and the crescent-shaped bread that had become fashionable since Marie Antoinette introduced it in France. It had been the creation of an Austrian baker celebrating the victory over the Ottomans. The tray itself was a contraption that George had commissioned in his own atelier, that balanced on foldout legs that straddled his body. He always preferred to start the day with the first meal in bed, settling into a review of the morning's *Journal de Paris*.[4]

Ignoring the report of the previous day's weather, as he had been able to familiarise himself directly with the fact that it had indeed been brisk and rainless, he skipped to the main announcement that morning, which was of a twenty-day mourning period at Versailles for the death of King Frederic II of Prussia. Everyone was prescribed black, although as a timid rebuke to the sobriety of the departed protestant king, the men were recommended silver swords and the ladies diamonds. A few unremarkable chemistry notices were followed by a long complaint from the Inspecteur General of the Buildings of the Duc of Orleans, who had not been consulted for a prior article on the church of Notre Dame, with grave consequences for the accuracy of said article. Even the report of Philippe Galopin—who almost lost his son as he lowered him upside down, holding him by his feet, his head dangling into the toxic fumes at the bottom of the well he had dug in one of the private residences in Paris—could not arouse George's interest. Although he did appreciate the scientific spirit of the ensuing

4 *Journal de Paris*, September 5, 1786.

experiment, when the father and the freshly resuscitated son lowered a bird in a cage into the well. The bird did not survive its descent.

George rejoiced that the Palais-Royal would see the premiere of a new set of comedies and might provide a reprieve from the continuation of the tedious opera *L'Heureux Stratagème*, which he had already suffered through the previous week. And finally, the combination of the announcements of the stock values, the exchange rates, and the lottery results always struck him as a happy juxtaposition. For George, the root cause of the variation in each of those values was indistinguishable and thoroughly random. He recalled debating this with Nicolas, who had pointed to the many ways that a wealthy gentleman might play each of those and thereby evade the yoke of chance. Social class always trumped luck, it seemed.

Having gained little wisdom, he called out, "Jacques, would you be so kind as to come and shave me and help me dress. Nothing too fine—I'll be at work all day."

"Of course, monsieur," Jacques replied, and went to fetch the necessary tools.

George settled on a straight oak chair as Jacques sharpened the shaving knife on a strap hanging from a brass knob. A large mirror hung opposite, allowing him to observe the pleasurable ritual. With proportionally short legs, George only appeared taller than his merely average height when sitting. His tailor compensated for his disproportion by very slightly raising the level of the waist in his coats. His frame was thin and muscular, fitting a vigorous forty-year-old. A narrow scar on his left cheekbone was a relic of a highly kinetic youth. Jacques began to shave him, raising an eyebrow in scrutiny when nearing the old wound as he always did—he had to take more care with the blade when going over the uneven texture that the scar presented.

"I have always been curious," Jacques said softly, continuing his work, "about this scar."

George, who had found himself in a somewhat reflective state on this day, was grateful for his curiosity. "I spent much time outside in my youth, occasionally falling out of trees, sometimes overestimating my ability to descend. At a particular fall, fleeing a rare misunderstanding with my twin sister, Violette, I had been far away from home, and during the long trek back, the wound had healed badly."

Jacques complimented him, saying that the scar provided a rugged accent to his otherwise elegant, almost aristocratic demeanour. George looked into the mirror to confirm this. A sharp nose accentuated a long face, bright blue eyes set against thick dark hair with more than the veil of grey that had emerged after Violette's sudden departure.

George, who had never thought of the scar in that regard and was warmed by his servant's perspective, continued to describe his youth to Jacques: "The woods were familiar, since before his accidental death my father had often taken me hunting. I had always found my father's excitement at the wanning warmth emanating from the stilted bodies of his prey disturbing. I had gained an early familiarity with handling the carcasses of the forest, but always mourned the loss of the force of nature that had been snuffed out by my father's gun. During one such hunt, my father was accidentally shot in the face by a fellow hunter shortly after he himself had downed a particularly large antler. Both died within minutes." George was quiet for a moment before asking, "Did you enjoy being outside in nature when you were a child, Jacques?"

"There was not much opportunity in the area of Paris where we lived, but a few times a year we would visit my father's mother in the village, two days' walk away. We always spent a night in the forest on the way there and on the way back. That was magical. The trees spoke to me at night, backlit by the moon. When we arrived, I would tell my grandmother their stories, and she always listened approvingly."

"Jacques," exclaimed George, "I did not know you were a romantic."

As he grew up, life and death, often side by side in nature, gradually became familiar to George. Indeed, it had always eerily aroused him to come across the decaying carcass of a rabbit or deer devoured by wolves or some other predator. That his own father could become part of this same pattern of nature was a shock, reaching beyond the acute pain of losing a parent, as distant as that parent might have been. In an evening discussion with Nicolas, George had speculated that the event of his father's violent death seemed to connect him to nature but in a manner that confused his empirical dedication as a nascent observing scientist. Nicolas and George had spent that long evening reflecting on their relation to what they observed in their role as scientists. It appeared to George that he was less independent of the observed than he had surmised. He had described to his friend how the connection had been through the senses, when he saw that the exhalation of animals attracted insects and that each insect was attracted by a different animal. Just as the flies preferred the dung of animals, as well as their carcasses, others savoured the pungent breath of the living. Meat-eating animals smelled differently from those who only consumed plants. A differencc hc had also learnt to discern in humans. He could always pick out the vegetarians by their smell, before he even heard how they considered that a man of the Enlightenment should refrain from eating meat.

"High time to get to work and see how Jeanne and Gaston have progressed. Why don't you stop by later when you head out to the market?" said George, as his thoughts now turned to the practical problem of embalming the zebra.

"Certainly. I will make a list of food, but we also need wax to polish the parquet floors," responded Jacques as George was already making his way through the double entrance door.

"And get some grease from the workshop for the door hinges," George called out from the landing. His face tingling from the friction of the shave, he sailed down the stairs, just missing a deliveryman who was headed to one of the upper-floor neighbours, carrying a large round box.

•

"Good morning, Monsieur George." Jeanne's voice rang out, eager and optimistic as the day was young, though she did not look up from her work. Her hair had been hurriedly tied with a narrow scrap leather strap from the workshop.

Jeanne was habitually the first in the atelier in the morning, and on this day, she was absorbed in a pile of sketches. She had laid out the zebra skin on the large oak table of the atelier. It had been carefully cut with a straight line from the anus to the mouth, with a double cross at each of the legs. From there, incisions ran down the length of each leg, albeit salvaging the hooves. The skin had been carefully skived by Gaston, to thin the skin and eliminate any traces of muscle so that it could absorb the tanning chemicals thoroughly.

Jeanne glanced up at George. "We've called for an ass to be brought to the studio this morning, so we can look more closely at the musculature," she told him. "I hope you don't object. And Gaston is already scraping the zebra's skin so we can start the conservation work."

"Very well—it is all in good hands, I see. I'll start the preparation of the chemicals."

While George was not overly secretive by nature, he still instinctively avoided making the recipe too easily accessible to Jeanne and Gaston, lest they find themselves someday in the atelier of one of his competitors. He retrieved from the cupboard against the outer wall a large glass bowl, rendered opaque from years of stirring and mixing.

George had learnt much from his master, Jean-Baptiste Bécoeur. Bécoeur had been a childhood friend of his father. Ever since saving the life of Louis XV, who was suffering from a bout of typhoid fever in August 1744 during a passage in Metz, Bécoeur's course to fame had been set. Though more through luck than skill, it nevertheless became known as the "miracle of Metz." His deep knowledge of pharmacopoeia penetrated the secrets of chemistry. His studies of poisons and drugs led him to his other passion, the conservation of animals.

Often, George's father had hunted the species that Bécoeur wanted to prepare. His father was able to make a kill with minimal traces, which was essential for displaying the animal in full grace. The giant antler that had been his father's last shot still adorned Bécoeur's atelier in Metz. He refused to sell it, and when George visited his mother, he would always pass by and place his hand on its long neck.

As a testament to his friendship with George's father, Bécoeur had confided to George the secret of his embalmment formula:

Camphor–5 ounces
Powdered arsenic–2 pounds
White soap–2 pounds
Tartar salt–12 ounces
Powdered lime–4 ounces

He had explained to George how to proceed. "Cut the soap in narrow slices, as fine as you can, and put them in a pot on a low fire, stirring constantly. When it has melted completely, add the salt and the lime. Take the pot off the fire and carefully spread the arsenic over the mix. Gently stir the whole before adding the camphor. Be sure to grind it finely beforehand, adding a little bit of alcohol. The final paste should have the consistency of glue. The best way to store it is in a glass pot or even a clay one."[5]

As George mixed his own paste in the large glass bowl, he recounted those instructions, as he did every time he prepared it. Though he knew the recipe by heart, there was a pleasing comfort in murmuring Bécoeur's words to himself, as if summoning him from obscurity.

Bécoeur had also shown him how to prepare the skin and shape its posture. The resulting mix filled an oak tanning drum where the skin would soak, with Gaston dutifully stirring the brew every few hours.[6]

With rabbits, foxes, minks, hedgehogs, and even a lonely African galago inhabiting an oak cabinet on the far side of the room, the workshop was quite a menagerie. Next to it, on a matching cabinet, perched birds of all sizes, ranging from practice projects such as pigeons and ducks, to an exquisite pink flamingo balancing on a thin leg reinforced with a steel bar, a toucan with its extraordinary beak, five bright green small parrots, and several sombre barn owls.

George took pride in the fact that the larger, more prestigious commissions had all left the workshop, often to the Jardin du Roi—albeit with a twinge of regret at them being out of his

5 Thiney, 2014, p. 58.

6 Actual vegetable tanning takes several months, but I have taken liberty with time in service of the narrative.

sight forever. The royal collection of naturalised animals was most impressive, not least because of the efforts of his atelier.

The Comte de Buffon had been the director of the Jardin du Roi for the past forty-seven years. Now in his twilight days, the author of *l'Histoire Naturelle* and prominent member of the Académie des sciences continued to be an important sponsor. The prior week, Buffon had visited the rue des Saints-Pères. The old man had sat, sprawling his legs in the large leather chair in the corner of the atelier. With the booming voice of a man with few doubts on his position in the world, he reflected to George: "A life spent at the service of the natural sciences gave me a nostalgic affection for the smells of workshops such as yours. The staleness of the skins competing with the sharp aroma of the camphor, sweetened by soap, and enveloped by alcohol vapours!"

In a state of great excitement, he read to George a most extraordinary letter addressed to him, by the American ambassador, Thomas Jefferson. "'Sir—I had the honour of informing you some time ago that I had written to my friends in America, desiring they would send me such of the spoils of the moose, caribou, elk and deer as might throw light on that class of animals; but more particularly to send me the complete skeleton, skin, and horns of the moose, in such condition as that the skin might be sowed up and stuffed on its arrival here.'"[7]

"An exciting perspective, Monsieur le Comte," George said, "but may I enquire what prompted the ambassador to such an act?"

---

7 This occurred a year later, in 1787. Source: Jefferson, "From Thomas Jefferson to Buffon."

Buffon, adjusting himself to sit more upright in the chair, explained: "At a recent dinner I had taken the position with Ambassador Jefferson that Europe's animals were superior to America's because they were bigger. I told him that I believed America to be insufferably warm, with small animals, and populated with inhabitants with a low libido. Ignoring the third, granting the partial truth of the first point, Jefferson had tried to rebut at least the second proposition, over several conversations. You see, Jefferson is not like his predecessor Franklin, who could conduct a conversation with the expected wit and eloquence. He is a brilliant but somewhat dour American. In any case, not being able to win the argument at the table, the ambassador then wrote to General John Sullivan asking him to hunt down the largest moose, caribou, deer, and elk he could find, then skin and ship them together with their skeletons to Paris where they could be further treated.[8] It was an odd assignment for Sullivan, who was one of the heroes of the American war, serving under von Steuben, the German who drilled discipline into the revolutionary forces, overcoming their objection of being led by an openly homosexual man."[9]

"Only Americans could be concerned about such inclinations. In France, it would not be objectionable," quipped George, adding (to please his host and betraying his own convictions), "at least for a general."

---

8 Adams, 2000, p. 132.

9 "The Revolutionary War Hero," History.

"Indeed, not an issue for a general indeed!" Buffon exclaimed with an enthusiasm that drowned in a fit of coughing that had him grasping the arms of the chair. "The remains of the great beasts have just arrived at the Jardin du Roi."

Aside from the curious origin of the animals, George rejoiced at many months of fascinating work ahead, albeit with much debate. Buffon was not a man to accept defeat, and George expected pressure to make the American animals appear smaller—or at least exhibit them in such a way as not to make them too impressive. Fortunately, Buffon's visit had occurred before the queen's zebra was delivered; the Comte de Buffon had left before the crate arrived.

"We narrowly sidestepped a diplomatic incident!" George exclaimed to his assistants. "Given Buffon's involvement with the French zebra in Versailles, it is prudent to keep him away from the British one."

Jeanne participated by letting out an audible sigh of relief. George imagined her to be slightly bewildered by the European political ramifications associated with her new role in the atelier and not entirely grasping the consequences.

While Gaston proceeded to treat the zebra's skin with the prepared liquid, Jeanne and George strolled out into the courtyard, where a light autumn drizzle was making the granite cobblestones shine. The wooden beams supporting the short roof that partly covered the open area flanking the gate displaced a glistening green structure from the flaking of paint. George noted that this needed to be repaired, as his visitors should be conveyed an impression of perfection and great attention to detail. On the walls under the awning, there was a line of iron rings to tie down horses. One of them held a long-frayed rope, leading to a brooding donkey, standing still, seemingly at peace with its condition.

"So essentially what we want is to capture the difference between the ass and the zebra," Jeanne said while straightening her glasses on her nose and firmly anchoring her hands below her ribs. The tilt of her head and way of raising an eyebrow fleetingly echoed Violette's mannerisms, leaving a matte bubble in George's chest.

"That's right. So what do you observe?" George asked while he walked towards the donkey. "What is it that defines the wildness of the zebra and the submissiveness of an ass?"

"There is the drooping eyelid of the ass, its slightly bowed head suggesting submission, perhaps the lack of tension in its back, the position of the tail that hangs more than that of a zebra?"

"Indeed, and it misses the sparkle in its eye that projects independence and rebellion. It is what we as humans identify with. It is why Buffon was obsessed with taming the Versailles zebra. He considers its resistance an offence to the superiority of man over the animal realm. It almost seems personal, as if the great naturalist had an account to settle with nature. His tragedy is that, while an extraordinary observer of nature, his thoughts were always bound by a strong conviction that everything has a direct cause and that man rises above everything," George stated with vehemence. He resented being excluded by birth from the royal premises where these experiments were conducted. "When we think of our own free will, our unique ability to shake the shackles that bind us—that's what we look for in the wildness of nature. That is what the queen should see in her zebra."

"What about the legs?"

"I don't think they're necessarily that different, although the zebra must look more athletic, appearing to bound away at any moment, rather than to stand still and wait for its master to instruct it. We should highlight the tension in the legs, but the musculature is fundamentally similar."

"Should we dissect it?" asked Gaston, who had stepped outside to observe the donkey alongside them.

"I think we can spare our friend here," said Jeanne with some compassion. "Perhaps at least this one can be granted a natural end."

George nodded in agreement. "Indeed, animals deserve our empathy, and God knows enough have perished for the very purpose of coming through the gates of our atelier. It is sensitive of you to be concerned."

"Let's get a cat!" exclaimed Jeanne, her face brightening.

George had come to appreciate her spontaneous, if not always relevant, outbursts—it was the same vein of child-like impulsiveness, he imagined, that fuelled her creativity. "Perhaps," he said gently, "but for now we should turn to the work at hand. I want to emphasise that it is the impression of the whole we are after, and we have a good idea of the parts from anatomic drawings that are readily available. The wildness is not expressed in the individual muscles, tendons, or skeleton."

Jeanne turned to Gaston. "I have already built the wooden backbone for the zebra, around which I can sculpt the animal with rope and wax. I plan to reproduce the zebra's skin on heavy linen, so that I can drape it over the structure and see whether it works. That way it won't damage or wear the actual skin."

"Rope and wax, excellent," Gaston replied. "Let's not go back to the massive wooden sculptures. Louis XV's rhinoceros weighed a ton, and it did not help to express any detail. It has become impossible to move."[10]

"At least no one will steal the rhinoceros!" quipped Jeanne.

Chuckling, George observed, "Indeed that beast was a bad idea. Fortunately, we now know better how to conduct our profession, and our zebra will be light as a feather."

10 The rhinoceros of Versailles actually died in 1793.

3

The Rights of Humans

George had spent the greater part of the day in his rooms, comforted that things were progressing satisfactorily and reviewing the accounts of his firm. He had briefly worried about Jeanne, whose life was almost entirely defined by her work in the atelier—at least to the best of his knowledge—before his thoughts turned to the evening conversation ahead with Nicolas at the Café de Foy. As customary, his valet Jacques had prepared George's attire for the outing: a grey silk coat with a green ribbon lining the length of the opening and the split on the back, ivory buttons hinting at his profession, and an exuberantly ruffled shirt protruding over the low-cut opening of a striped vest. Virginal white silk stockings in a pair of plain black shoes set with a narrow silver buckle aided in completing the ensemble. The otherwise sober dark green felt hat featured a small bright parrot feather.

George entered the Palais-Royal from the rue de Montpensier, past the ramshackle Variétés Palais-Royal theatre that had been hastily assembled along with the Camp des Tartares construction that separated the courtyard from the palace itself, facing the Louvre on its front side. Both buildings had primarily been constructed to raise some early income for the construction of the Palais-Royal complex as the Duc d'Orléans's funds had dwindled—the capital requirements of the real estate developer dwarfed even the exuberant lifestyle of the feasting nobleman.

Since he had seen a neighbouring house burn to the ground as a ten-year-old, George sometimes worried that wooden assemblies placed side by side were a disaster waiting to happen, at the whim of a candle tumbled by a careless elbow. As soon as it opened, there were already plans to replace the Variétés with a vast and opulent new building. The Palais-Royal had become a hive of entertainment, distraction, and fantasy of all kinds, and there seemed to be an insatiable appetite for more and bigger halls. Yet the Camp des Tartares remained and served as a Parisian bazar housing several dozen shops proposing trinkets, clothes, or books.[11] A few political twists and turns later, silver or golden earrings in the shape of a guillotine might be all the rage. Now, for five sols, he had admired the beautiful Zulima, a nymph whose attraction had remained undimmed, even after a reported two hundred years in the public eye. Her long blond hair covered her breast, whose waxed surface would

11 It was torn down in 1830.

be bared for more coins, all as an enticement to migrate to the live girls in the next rooms.

Avoiding the bustle and the pickpockets of the Camp des Tartares, George headed around the building into the crowd down the one hundred arcades of the Galerie de Montpensier, at the end of which was his destination. At this time of day, the galleries were already crowded. Officers in full uniform mingled with provincial thrill seekers who would be fortunate to lose only their money: bankers, writers, musicians, politicians, aristocrats. Crowning this constellation were the hundreds of women who plied their trade under the galleries. The lowest tier of girls solicited their clients in the gardens or under the galleries, luring them with *dévoilés*, deeply cut dresses, and hair elaborately architected with braided coloured ribbons. Although particularly elegant, they did not always stand out in the crowd of refined women who huddled under the galleries. To erase any doubt, many wore a ring in the shape of a heart, sometimes decorated with a cameo of Venus. They would take their clients to the *sous-sols*—or basements—of certain cafés or to rooms in the neighbourhood, often decorated with erotic drawings, velvet curtains betraying traces of age, and a bed buried in plush cushions. Some made additional money by spying for the police who rewarded them as a rich information trove for the political intrigue that increasingly simmered under the surface. One of George's clients had finished his evening in the Palais-Royal bereft of his watch and wallet, as was not uncommon.

In the months after Violette's death, George had immersed himself in this underworld, following one harlot or another, or both. He would reward them generously, vaguely compensating them for the pain he was trying to bury through them. His grief remained unassailably present, but he did discover a whole new layer of the Parisian fabric. Cocotte, a particularly bright girl, had described to him the hidden infrastructure that the girls were subject to. Of the police they needed to bed for free to avoid arrest, of the rich who enjoyed exerting power over sexual enjoyment, and of the women who supplied the remedies for avoiding pregnancy or other herbs when the previous ones had failed. Unexpectedly, these interactions soothed his emotions more than any tryst, reconnecting George with the living.

One recent evening, from a doorway in one of the arches of the Galerie de Montpensier, Cocotte had called out to him. "Hey, Monsieur George," she trilled, "come see—I've got something to show you."

He knew that she wasn't soliciting his clientele, as their encounters had evolved from desperate fumbles to intimate conversations.

He followed her through the door, and to his surprise, she climbed the stairs ahead of him. In the obscurity only offset by the glow from the candles hanging from the vaulted ceiling outside, shining through the dirty window above the door, he could discern the rhythmic glow of the yellow satin hugging her derrière. On the top floor, she opened a door onto a diminutive attic room, with only a stool, bed, and side table, upon which stood a rudimentary basin and pitcher. A small, simple framed painting of a bathing nymph adorned the wall. She lit a candle and smiled at George with great expectation.

“Congratulations, Cocotte!” He was genuinely surprised and pleased at the development, one which he had long hoped for her. “You have a room inside the Palais—how wonderful! How did this happen?”

“A sad cause with a happy consequence: a colleague who rented this room was so severely beaten by the police a few weeks ago that she can no longer work. I’ve helped her out on several occasions, so she left me the lease. It’s a lot of money, but I can also get richer clients now, and couples who pay more, as it is more discreet to enter the gallery directly instead of escorting a girl out of the courtyard.”

“I’m really happy to hear that, but how are you?”

“It’s up and down, as always in this work. Sometimes there are genuine moments, when people are searching for something. Like it was with you the first times you came. You seemed so lost and eager for touch, on the flesh and also in the soul. Another woman comes to me regularly, a comtesse, I think, who seems fonder of my gender than of yours, but mostly she relishes having more control than her dominant comte allows her. She’s interesting. A character. I feel for her. Late in the evening, there are always inebriated men who have lost their higher faculties, if they ever had any to begin with.” She sighed. “Some days are better than others.”

“It’s good to see you and hear that you are well enough. You are so courageous. But I must apologise and take leave, as my friend Nicolas is waiting for me.” George dug into his pocket and removed the brass tube that held his money. “I’ve recently had good luck at the gambling tables across the courtyard, so wanted to leave you a contribution for the rent of your wonderful new space."

"Your habits have changed!" she exclaimed. "You always avoided gambling. One evening you even justified that with a story about mathematics, chance, and something about a Scotsman called Baise. All a bit complicated for me. Perhaps Mr. Baise helped you win?"

George smiled knowingly, and Cocotte thanked him profusely and walked down with him, taking her posting again outside the door.

An entirely different category of women sat on the terraces of the Café de Foy and led an opulent life with refined apartments on the floors immediately above the gallery. They would have several admirers with varying degrees of constancy, whom they would accompany to the theatre or the opera, being richly rewarded for their companionship.

Violette had always been amused by their seductive chatter. Although she never really engaged with them directly, she confided that she felt a stitch of jealousy for their freedom to misbehave, their colourful dresses, and their adventures. Together with his twin, he used to frequent the opera as well, much more often. Now when he entered the opera house, he felt the heavy emptiness where her arm used to weigh as her sparkling eyes reflected the crystals hanging down from the ceiling, lips the same red of the stage curtains. A whiff of dark ochre and light jasmine that made him want to walk closer to her and breathe deeply, so as to inhale her essence.

George shook his head to rid himself of the melancholy and dove back into the buzz of the pleasantries that this mixed crowd echoed under the vaulted ceilings, their shapes blending through the dancing lights of the modern oil lamps overhead. The recent addition of silver reflectors behind the flame, an invention of the Abbé Matherot de Perigny a dozen years earlier, had been an enormous improvement. Violette, upon seeing it, had exclaimed, "What a delightful innovation; such a clever use of mirrors." And George had concluded that nothing better could be invented in any future.[12]

The reading rooms were a unique feature of the Palais-Royal. For a fixed monthly rent, one could consult fashionable books or newspapers in a heated and well-lit room. This became such a prominent way to reach readers that some books were printed in multiple short volumes with the reading-room public in mind, so that they could be consumed more easily.

Violette would often spend entire winter days in the reading room, taking in the books that were not readily accessible in their province. She would return to the rue des Saints-Pères and rush up to share with George what she had discovered. Her literary appetite was voracious. "It seems so unfair that Dante houses the great Greek philosophers in hell, even if only the first circle, just because they had the bad luck of being born before our Saviour!" she exclaimed one day. Montesquieu had

---

12 *Nature*, "History of Public Lighting in Paris," (132) 1933, p. 888.

been another discovery and made her question the role of the king, echoing the murmurs in the refined salons of Paris.

Another time, somewhat perplexed, she swung open the apartment door exclaiming that Jean de la Fontaine was not the century-old moralist she had been taught about. "'Master Crow was perched on a tree, Master Crow held a cheese in his beak,'" she recited, then added, "but they never told us about his extensive writings on libertines, louts, and lechers!"

Laughing heartedly at her delighted indignation, he quoted the poet back to her. "'Beware, so long as you live, of judging men by their outward appearance.'"

Publishers and bookshops lined the galleries; George passed François-Charles Gattey's publishing shop, then Joseph Pain's bookshop, Les trois bossus. After he had been too liberal for his time, Gattey was to perish under the guillotine for printing work that was no longer liberal enough, soon followed by his unrestrained sister who imprudently shouted "Vive le Roi" during her brother's very short trial. Violette had commended her for her bravery. The briskness of the siblings' deaths was in such sharp contrast to the gentle fading of George's sister. Just one chop, heads detached, end of thoughts and existence. His sister had suffered for an infinite week, slowly losing her coordination, the depths of her thoughts fading. The animals he prepared had died with more resignation and dignity.

Noticing that his pace had stalled, George proceeded down the gallery. A crowd was lining up at number seven—the Salon Curtius—where for only a few sols anyone could experience dinner at Versailles. Philip Curtius was born in Baden in 1737 and became a master sculptor of realistic wax figures. For a dozen sols, ticket holders could walk amongst wax renderings of dining aristocrats and even fondle their silk stockings or caress their mink collars. Curtius's daughter Anna would marry a François Tussaud. They would both immigrate to London in 1802 and continue the family tradition by founding a wax museum.

Further down, number fifty-three hosted a puppet theatre under the name of the Italian Fantoccinis, run by Monsieur Castagna. Here, wooden puppets could be observed executing complex dances for an audience of three hundred. In the breaks, mandolin players or singers would entertain the audience. Leaving the theatre with Nicolas one afternoon, he had commented on how mesmerising this invented, artificial world could be, having no other subject than itself, yet perfectly entertaining.

Next to it, the Petits Comédiens de Son Altesse Sérénissime Monseigneur le Comte de Beaujolais was inaugurated in October 1784 and presented another curious and popular form of entertainment. Children soon replaced the original puppets and mimed a performance while their voices were spoken by actors behind the curtain. Eight hundred theatregoers were distracted from the harshness of Parisian life, night after night, by dozens of actors, dancers, and musicians. The formidable Marguerite Brunet, taking the name of Montansier, took over the theatre for the large sum of 560,000 francs.[13] At a young

---

13 Montansier actually took over on June 15, 1789.

age, following a first love to the Americas, and then another to Martinique, she found her footing as a businesswoman on Saint Domingue, trading cloth. Returning to Paris, she opened a gaming parlour, directing her first theatre in Versailles, then in various provinces before taking her enterprise to the Palais-Royal. She immediately doubled the capacity of the theatre to 1,300 seats, and scheduled light plays for sold-out audiences. Living above the theatre, she had the wisdom to steer clear of politics where the gathering clouds were palpable, as she could monitor from the conversations of the thousands of visitors passing through her institution.

Across the courtyard, less familiar to George, the Galerie de Beaujolais hosted the few dozen gaming parlours where fortunes were gambled on a whim, alternated by the clubs such as the Salon des Arts with exhibitions and music. Next to it was the Assemblée Militaire for officers, the Masonic Société Olympique, and the Société des Colons—a refuge reserved for those with overseas possessions—and the Club Politique.

George reached the Café de Foy, situated just before the newly opened Café Méchanique where each table had an ingenious mechanism with two tubes in its base. The first one served to lower orders to the kitchen below, then moments later a tray with food would rise through the second tube to the awe of the unsuspecting guest. Others admired the operations through the bay windows from the outside. The Café de Foy itself had been founded in 1725 in the adjoining street and now spread over five arcades in the Palais-Royal.

The Café de Foy was renowned for its fine table. The owner had been the first to get permission for a garden terrace in front. Actresses and courtisanes familiarised themselves with the intrigues or twists of favour amongst the assembled wealthy patrons of the café.

It was here that George had tasted fresh oysters for the first time, together with Violette after a theatre outing, as they had stopped for a late-night dinner. George had squeezed some lemon juice onto the shells for both of them. Violette's cheeks slightly contracted in the expectation of their acidity, and although familiar with the gelatinous consistency of many parts of the animal realm, they had looked at each other with some trepidation at the thought of having it on their tongues. Rapidly, they both slithered the oysters from their shell beds. George recalled his sister's look of sensual bliss as they grabbed each other's hand across the table in excitement.

In the entresol above the Café de Foy was an exclusive chess club. Nicolas had mentioned that Talleyrand had recently won thirty thousand francs at a game table. As he crossed the threshold, George renewed his wonderment at the inextricable connection of luxury to pleasure and to a dollop of licentiousness. Seemingly entirely superficial and hedonistic, the Palais-Royal was nevertheless the feeding ground of the Enlightenment ideas that swirled around Paris. In contrast, a severity of norms in the provinces seemed to lead to simplicity of taste and paucity of ideas. He briefly entertained the thought that this inference might merely be a self-serving justification of a decadent society heading for a libertine cliff, until he glimpsed Nicolas at a table in the back in the company of Pierre de Courbetin. He walked over to join them.

Standing tall at one meter seventy-five, his friend the Marquis Nicolas de Condorcet had chestnut hair, with a sharp nose, wide forehead, and round chin, or as the duchesse d'Abrantès had once described him: "His figure, without being noticeably beautiful, made a striking impression. His forehead was vast and curved, his eyes deep, his nose eagle-like and very pronounced; his mouth was the most characteristic trait of his appearance; his smile was calm but easily betrayed satire. The only hint of intimacy in his expression was when the corners of his mouth were raised in mockery, reflecting the intense feelings behind a thought coolly voiced."

Nicolas struggled to stand straight, out of shyness rather than physical limitation. In 1775, his face had been slightly scarred by smallpox. A poor talker, his preference for reading and writing, rather than expounding, was a serious handicap for success in eighteenth-century France, as the debates in the various salons were the foundation of one's social reputation. Still, Condorcet was a memorable presence—when he did speak, he could always broaden an argument by showing how it connected to other arguments, steering discussions away from simplistic conclusions.

George's friendship with Nicolas was an unlikely one. A shared inquisitiveness comfortably bridged the gap in their social status. George and Nicolas echoed each other's aloofness, and although they both knew its price, they could never quite prioritise making this a topic of discussion between them, respecting an implicit code of male friendships—or at least this was how George interpreted their mutual understanding.

George wound his way through the Café du Foy, then settled himself in a chair at his friend's table. "We were born on the same day," George observed whimsically.

"Are you being nostalgic?"

"I mean my actual birthday. Jeanne Bécu was born on the same day as I, on August nineteenth in 1743. And she is sitting at a table by the far side window, with six others. It is the table that looks out on the colonnade." George tipped his head in the general direction.

"Madame du Barry?"[14] Nicolas chuckled. "That's funny. I had not realised you were the exact same age. But she should have had her lover stuffed by you, just to celebrate your equivalence!"

"That is not funny. She is certainly not aware of my birthday, nor of my existence," George said with mock indignance. "And as for stuffing her royal lover, that would have been the end of me, since Louis XV died of smallpox and was soaked in alcohol and lime before being quickly shipped off to Saint-Denis. The chemist of Versailles told me that he wasn't even given the chance to embalm him, although he also counted himself lucky by dodging a likely infection."

---

14 Madame du Barry—née Jeanne Bécu—was King Louis XV's lover from 1769 to 1774, after Madame de Pompadour had retired from the position. She was of simple origins and by all accounts ravishingly beautiful. She also turned out to have a remarkable moral compass under the circumstances, but was also the subject of endless intrigues, and was known to be a proliferate spender. When Louis XVI succeeded the throne, his wife, Marie Antoinette, saw to it that she was immediately banned from court and society.

"Yes, well in any case, the threat of Marie Antoinette's wrath made sure that Jeanne Bécu left Versailles before the king died. Marie Antoinette was lucky to have had a mild case as a child, which protected her, unlike her brother and sisters. Twelve years ago, she convinced her husband to have an inoculation, as well as gave it to her own children. Really quite courageous given the opposition to smallpox inoculation by the conservative faction at court. It is surprising du Barry did not catch it. In any case, I'm not sure how she ended up at the Café de Foy tonight."

From the other side of their table, Pierre had been staring across the room while Nicolas and George were bantering about the comtesse. George, Nicolas, and Pierre had been friends for over a decade and occasionally met for dinner at the Café de Foy. Pierre had become increasingly reclusive as his difficulties piled up. His youthful traits had receded under a grey skin tone that seemed to envelop his entire being. A black coat added to the gloomy appearance, along with the silver streaks competing for attention in his curly hair. The lustre from the fine silk of the fabric of his frock glistened as he moved, and its undulating golden trim recalled the dandy he had been. The tidy sum inherited from his father was no longer adequate to fund the lifestyle that he had grown accustomed to. He had spent much of it on idle pleasures, but also in pursuit of his interest in the history of the royal family. He owned a vast library with seemingly every text written about the rulers back to Clovis. His slight but consistent stutter continued to be an obstacle in a society where fluid conversation, specked with puns or literary allusions, was highly prized—George could not help but find it original. Pierre regularly published critical, but always painfully accurately researched, editorials about the monarchy. So naturally, he knew every detail about Madame du Barry's vertiginous path through society.

"Ah, did you all know she is the illegitimate daughter of a se-se-seamstress?" Pierre informed them, having noticed whom they were observing. "And that both Jeanne Bécu and Jeanne d'Arc were born in Vaucouleurs? Remarkable, as one would save France and the other hasten its decline." Pierre laughed out loud. "I read the memoirs of the Prince de Ligne, and he described her as 'tall, well proportioned, a se-se-seducing blond, long forehead, beautiful eyes, fine eyelashes, an oval face with mirrored dimples on each cheek that made her uniquely charming: smiling lips, a fine skin, with a bosom to reproach the world.'"[15]

George grinned at the description and looked over to see Nicolas was equally amused.

The later Madame du Barry had grown up a ravishingly beautiful young woman. Her strict and sober education at the Convent of Saint-Aure had fallen well short of its ambition, at least in its moral dimension. After a few odd occupations, ranging from selling trinkets to being a dame de compagnie for a wealthy lady, she had joined the ranks of the Paris prostitutes, working at Madame Quisnoy's brothel-casino. What might have been a slow descent into social oblivion instead

15 Haslip, 1992, p. 34.

turned out to be the foundation for soaring to the pinnacle of French society. The casino's owner and well-known procurer du Barry spotted her. He installed her in his household and opened the doors to Parisian society. Her beauty and natural charm conquered ministers and courtiers, as well as men of the church.

The Maréchal de Richelieu, forty-five years her senior, was one of her most faithful and recurring lovers or clients, depending on one's perspective. A military man, de Richelieu had expelled the British from Menorca, occupied Hannover, and assaulted the Prussians. Having known Louis XV since his childhood and later becoming an intimate friend, de Richelieu was adept at court and even more at courting. Reputedly Choderlos de Laclos based his Valmont in *Les Liaisons dangereuses* on the maréchal.

Pierre continued his gossip. "In any case, Louis had spotted Jeanne, became her lover, and installed her at Versailles. A pragmatic marriage of convenience to du Barry's brother, the Comte du Barry, had provided her with instant no-no-no-nobility. Thus Jeanne, the lowly daughter of a seamstress from the provinces, became the royal mistress."

Nicolas interrupted Pierre. "I have been a regular guest at the property of Couteulx de la Noraye, her neighbours at Louveciennes, but never met her there. At a dinner of one of her liaisons, the Duc de Brissac—which Nicolas and I attended—she had been expected, but instead sent a note of being indisposed at the last moment. I recall a memorable discussion, with Choderlos de Laclos, Germaine Necker—now

Madame de Staël—and the American ambassador.[16] Choderlos had borne the full gale of Madame de Staël's formidable youthful intellect. *Les Liaisons dangereuses* had been published by the former general only four years earlier, and its scandalous documentation of seduction and sexual passion as a tool of both power and pleasure had further opened Germaine's mind to the allure of a libertine life. The presence of the author had allowed her to explore the full potential of such machinations."

"Can you see what necklace she is wearing?" asked George somewhat mischievously and to retrieve the conversation from its wanderings.

"No such luck," countered Pierre. "A simple string of diamonds, although perfectly charming."

George remembered how the scandal of the other diamond necklace had enthralled all of Paris earlier in the year. Fourteen years earlier, Louis XV had ordered the jewellers Boehmer and Bassenge to make a necklace for Jeanne's delightful neck, at the outrageous price of two million livres. However, the king had died before it was finished, and its extravagance meant that it had remained unsold. As the daughter of an Austrian empress, Marie Antoinette did not want a necklace designed and intended for Jeanne, who was in her eyes nothing more than the low-birth mistress of her husband's predecessor and grandfather.

A motley crew of confidence tricksters had subsequently managed to take delivery of the necklace by impersonating

16 In reality, this particular dinner took place much later, around 1793, when Governor Morris had taken over from Thomas Jefferson. I have taken liberty to make a connection with Madame de Staël, whom Condorcet had indeed known.

the queen.[17] They disassembled it and sold the stones in London. Although Marie Antoinette was blameless, it further tarnished her reputation in the eyes of the population and eroded confidence in her husband, King Louis XVI. A steady supply of rumours and innuendo would continue to damage the name of l'Autrichienne.

"Still, wearing a diamond necklace in public shows a rebellious streak that I thought would have been suppressed by the need to conform and attempt to regain the approval of a society that would have her banished permanently to the Château de Louveciennes. It should have been an elegant retreat for 'devotion, penitence and mortification' as our rather dour American friend John Adams once wrote.[18] Good for her to ignore them," observed George.

Betraying his interest in engineering, George added, "Although I never understood how one could live at Louveciennes with the roaring and infernal Machine de Marly next to it, loudly pumping water from the Seine uphill all the way to the fountains of Versailles, some forty leagues away and almost five hundred feet up."

"Our standards for political reflection appear to be dropping! Fencing stolen goods is hardly the st-st-stuff of revolutions," retorted Pierre.

"Yes, yes—you're right of course," acquiesced George, leaning back in his chair.

---

17 The story became known as the affair of the Collier de la Reine and is chronicled in a novel by Alexandre Dumas.

18 Adams, 2000, p. 245.

Mathilde Joussereau stopped by their table, in the habitual whirlwind tour of her patrons. Her pride in the newly reopened establishment was visible to all. George had once been told how the reputation of her beauty had attracted Louis Philippe to the café in the rue Richelieu a decade earlier and guaranteed her a move to a prime location in the Galerie de Montpensier of the Palais-Royal, as well as a steady flow of prominent guests. Louis Philippe, Louis XVI's brother, had incurred the wrath of his noble kin by stooping to become a property developer by building the vast rectangular Palais-Royal behind the family palace that he had inherited.[19] The project had been a close call financially, and he was compelled to sell in London the prodigious art collection from the old palace.[20] George had admired the grand illustrated catalogue that had circulated widely in Paris at the time, but anything from the collection was far beyond his reach. Now the Palais-Royal had become a societal lightning rod, while it shaped the mores of the modern elite.

Mathilde was gifted with pencil-thin, always brightly painted lips that spread widely across an elongated face, high cheekbones lit with a dash of rouge on a powdered face, fiery brown eyes that betrayed a restless curiosity, and curly chestnut hair. Her right earlobe was torn because of a late-night heist when a robber had pulled off one of her earrings, shredding the flesh with it. Fortunately, fashion had evolved along with

---

19 After the Revolution, as a member of the new parliament, the now-named Philippe Egalité cast the one vote majority to send his brother to the guillotine.

20 Louis Philippe sold the collection in London in 1791—many of the paintings found their way into what is now the British Museum, founded in 1824. Source: Panzanelli, 2007.

Mathilde's social standing, and she now wore the more fashionable clip-ons, a sprinkling of small emeralds obscuring the torn ear George knew to be hiding behind the accessory.

The secret of the café's success was that Madame Joussereau was quite the scholar. An extensive familiarity with modern philosophers and societal commentators allowed her to engage in intellectual jousts with her clients. She was particularly admiring of Voltaire and hoped he might appear in the café someday, and that she might taste his acid wit for herself. Amidst the kaleidoscope of social norms that shaped the habits of the Palais-Royal, Mathilde was known to be concentrated mostly on making her café the favourite haunt of her patrons. For now, it flattered George to think that he was one of her favourite regular clients—and she always made it a priority to stop at his table, somewhat clumsily hiding a more than professional interest.

"I see you noticed the necklace," she said to George. "The papers will be abuzz tomorrow. The real tragedy is that du Barry did not have the intellectual interests of her more illustrious predecessor Madame de Pompadour, or France might well have been much different. The current court at Versailles is not even aware of the ideas that are boiling in Paris today. Quesnay, Diderot, Voltaire, d'Alembert—from economists to mathematicians, so many great minds connected to the state through the interventions of de Pompadour. And the comtesse's legacy is a tawdry jewellery scandal that she did not even have a role in!"

"Are you familiar with who is in her company tonight?" George asked.

Mathilde knew her clientele. "The comtesse keeps eclectic company, mostly nobles who, like her, have been rejected by the court. Sometimes by bad luck, as in her case, or prompted by their own actions."

Nicolas added, "The man on her left, with the yellow waistcoat, white *écharpe*, sharp nose, and wide demeanour was the Marquis de Honfleur, who provoked one of the favourites of the queen in a duel and committed the imprudent gaucherie of killing him. He has since been less than welcome in the salons of our circles."

"Yes, that was an unfortunate aim," continued Mathilde. "Next to him is the Comte de Beaubourg, whose unhappy circumstances made him such a strong proponent of capital punishment for the slightest offences that he even lost the patronage of the justice minister when he repeatedly criticised the court's lenience in his writings. As you see, Beaubourg is an excessively tall man, towering at one meter ninety-five. He always hunches, as if hunkering to be closer to other men. I'm told he led a lonely youth as the only child in an estranged household, reportedly spending much time outside with horses from the family stable. It didn't help that the priest who provided him with an education had not limited himself to matters of the mind."

"It sounds like this Beaubourg had a sad start in life," George speculated. "His most joyous memories must have been of riding out alone amongst the fields, galloping away from things rather than towards anywhere in particular."

Nicolas apparently also knew of the man. "Francois de Beaubourg's reputation had never fully recovered from a financial affair that saw the ruin of several prominent families from Lyon. You see, Beaubourg had provided capital to a few farmers who had been able to gain ownership of their land from impoverished nobles. Planted with wine stock, their businesses had thrived but had remained controversial, as threats to the social order. While the aristocracy often shied away from industrial activity, they considered the exploitation of the land to be their exclusive domain, rooted in a millenary tradition. The Comte de Beaubourg's loans undermined the way of the world, and they applied considerable pressure to cancel the loans. The resulting collapse left everyone worse off."

"Have you seen the lady to the left of him before—in the red dress and even redder rubies?" enquired Nicolas.

Flushing with feigned indignation, Mathilde explained, "She is a talented dancer from the opera, and very well read. I sometimes organise quiet soirees for the ladies who are more often valued for their horizontality than for the convincing nature of their arguments. Angélique d'Hannetaire is a bright spark, and I recall being fascinated with her ideas on how justice could be better meted out. The two other gentlemen I have not seen here before."

The discussions at the table of the comtesse were conducted in a particularly loud tone and carried across the room, partly stimulated by the copious coupes of champagne spread across the damask amongst the plates of oysters, but also fuelled by the shared societal reproach that had become etched into their personalities. The irrepressible urge to set the record straight caused their voices to rise, so that an absent authority might overhear that they had been wronged.

"God's word is abundantly clear that crimes must be punished harshly and with equal retribution. Exodus, Leviticus even twice, Deuteronomy, Matthew, and Romans all mandate that a life should be avenged with a life, an eye with an eye—and God put the government in place to carry that out. There can be no doubt!" Beaubourg exclaimed.

"But did not God give man faculties of reason, so that he might evaluate what actions are most effective?" countered Honfleur. George smiled at the rebuke.

"And deviate from God's word?"

"Zigzag—or *zickzack* as the Germans say—we meander all the time," said Honfleur, his face reddening noticeably to the edge of his high hairline. "It works for the defence walls of our cities, and it can work for our morals."

Mademoiselle d'Hannetaire straightened her stance and volunteered that Cesare Beccaria would have disagreed with both men.

"Wasn't he that Milanese marquis who spent a few weeks in Paris some years ago but did not make much of an impression? Morellet translated his little book, I recall," opined Beaubourg.

"He greatly impressed Catherine the Great as well as our new American ambassador, Thomas Jefferson."

Beaubourg raised a finger to object. "Of course—but not France. And what did Beccaria understand that you think we do not?"

The young lady explained, "It seems that while he remains congruent with God's word, he recommends a system for establishing punishment that helps our current world and not merely the next one."

"Just how does he propose to do that?" Beaubourg asked, a snide smile on his lips.

"It has been a few years since I studied it, but I recall that his views revolved around the social contract between the individual and society." Mademoiselle d'Hannetaire lowered her voice, and George strained to hear. "When men decide to act," she went on, "free in their will and rational in their steps, the goal of the justice system is to assist them so that these choices contribute to society. If they break a law or a habit, they should be punished swiftly, but also proportionally."

"Yes—an eye for an eye!" Beaubourg exclaimed.

Mademoiselle d'Hannetaire shook her head, setting into motion a considerable mass of stacked hair. George estimated that her age was not far over twenty, her face covered in white powder, sporting the easy confidence that beauty offered. Observing her from the side, he was struck by her nose resembling that of Greek statues, with a straight bridge, leading down to a narrow and wilful nose. "*Mais non*—proportionately does not mean equally. The punishment should be just enough to deter men from transgressing, but not harming them more than is strictly functional. It is the probability of punishment that is most important, not its severity. The goal is not vengeance but deterrence."

George watched as Honfleur, his face flushed with either champagne or irritability, leaned forward in his seat to object.

"The new habit of taking on the mantle of rationality does terribly impoverish our world. Room for feeling is eliminated, faith weakened, and the sexes become indistinguishable. Hardly an improvement just to avoid the odd head being lopped off."

"*Ma chère*, we are being terribly serious in our arguments this evening," Madame du Barry intervened with Angélique, clearly anticipating an imminent collision at her table, which George knew her time at court had taught her to deflect, in particular when the radical position was advocated by one of her own gender. George had seen Nicolas play this role and had marvelled at the selfless social grace that these interventions required. "Tell us about the opera you are soon performing in. I hear Monsieur Rameau has outdone himself."

A new company entered the Café de Foy, drowning out the discussion at the comtesse's table.

Having avidly followed the conversation at the comtesse's table from across the room, George turned his attention away from the group and towards his friend. "Nicolas, do I recall correctly that you met Beccaria?" he enquired. "You have mentioned him occasionally."

"I never had the honour of meeting him, as I was away in London when he came to Paris, but I have always been a great admirer of his *Dei delitti e delle pene*. We have corresponded regularly, and I dare say intensely. Beccaria had exhibited a great influence in his own country, where the Grand Duchy of Tuscany, just this year, abolished the death penalty. For him, justice is not merely a mechanism to control the public order, regardless of what personal tort has occurred—as the police only too often aim for. Beccaria argues that individuals have human rights, and that these need to be balanced with the concern for public order. You cannot simply arrest or even execute someone with the wider aim of quieting society, as is too often done today. There is a real trade-off that he draws attention to, for the first time, historically, I think. Beccaria particularly impressed officials and lawmakers and intellectuals from all camps, through his arguments to separate the roles of police and justice, to create some distance between the day-to-day friction in the street and the reflection that goes with the maintenance of the social contract. Echoing Beccaria, the British have implemented the idea that the accused should know what they are accused of and receive enough time to prepare a defence. This seems just and laudable, don't you agree?"

George nodded. "All too often, poor souls in Paris don't find out until they appear in front of the tribunal. A wonderful habit we have kept on from the Inquisition," he observed. "Can you even imagine yourself in that position?"

"Indeed, I can," said Pierre. "One of my valets recently was flogged one hundred times for an offence that he only found out about later, and with which he was not c-c-connected in any way. It is too often barbaric and only justified to set an example. Montesquieu wrote that every punishment that does not arise from absolute necessity is tyrannical."

Montesquieu, whom George knew to be principal in developing the theory of separation of powers, died during his youth. Nicolas had spoken of his deep regret in never having met the great man; he continued, "Beccaria suggested we reward virtue—and not just punish crime—noting that no country's law conceives of this. I am sure your employees, George, are more efficient rewarded than whipped?"

George smiled. "As I do not whip them but laud them when a beast is rendered particularly well, and since my enterprise is thriving, one might conclude that this is true enough—although I have not established the counterfactual and have no plan to!"

"Not entirely," intervened Nicolas. "Isn't it conceivable that the dread of being drowned in formaldehyde and frozen forever is the real deterrent for them?"

George laughed.

"The only thing we have proven is that we have exhausted our argument—and that Beccaria is a gr-gr-great man," concluded Pierre.

They left the Café de Foy earlier than usual and—even more unusually—headed straight home. Mathilde embraced Pierre and Nicolas at the door before turning to George. He noted that she was holding him imperceptibly longer than his friends and, upon saying his final goodbye, he suggested that they might see each other soon at a celebratory event at his workshop, where a surprise unveiling would occur.

4

Unveiling the Queen's Zebra

It had taken ten days of hard work, long evenings, and extensive debates to get the final expression of the zebra just right. George stared at its completed shape, doing a final assessment. Was it too muscular? Its head flexed too high? The eyelid tilted too far upward? The nose bridge too narrow? Its gait too wilful? In their quest for the right expression, George worried about overdoing it and creating a rococo travesty of the force of nature. But now, observing every detail, he believed that Jeanne had truly outdone herself. The zebra was ready for a private unveiling to which a small group of friends had been invited. It was a festive occasion but one that George knew needed to be handled discreetly due to the stature of the zebra's owner, and to avoid any unnecessary publicity. The tensions between France and England had recently increased and George was keen not to sleepwalk into a diplomatic incident.

The atelier had been transformed to receive the guests—through Jeanne's endeavours. The cabinets with the stilted animals remained prominently on display, cleverly lit with a set of mirrors and lenses that focussed the light from the many candelabra. The sturdy oak table that Jeanne and Gaston usually laboured at had been moved aside and covered with a thick green damask cloth lined with gilded tassels. On it, two large marble vases contained sweeping chestnut branches in autumnal colours, laden with its fruits peeking out with auburn glow from their green prickly envelopes, mixed with the late bloom of orange dahlias, interspersed with bright yellow rudbeckias. The ageing but serviceable harpsichord that George was allowed to borrow from his neighbour had been moved into the atelier. A musician from one of the Palais-Royal music halls had been retained.

In the middle of the room stood the zebra. Jeanne swept past George and hurriedly but delicately threw a white silk cloth over it, and the material gracefully collapsed around the zebra, closely hugging its hide and hinting at the underlying muscular curvature.

George abandoned his last-minute scrutiny and moved outside, where he welcomed his guests in the courtyard as they walked in or emerged from their carriages. Condorcet was there of course, as was the Comte de Buffon. It struck George that although both men were vastly different in age, they shared a quiet determination in their bearing that was hard to trace to a physical trait. He made a note to revisit this and explore how to add such expression to the beasts he prepared. Although not a friend of George's by any definition, the court scientist was the essential core of the naturalist community. In deference to the octogenarian, he was provided with a prominent seat. George had invited several of his neighbours, who he knew quietly endured the vile odours that sometimes emanated from the workshop, as well as a handful of botany students and several professors from the Sorbonne. Mathilde Joussereau's flowing grass-green silk dress contrasted with the rouge lighting her cheeks; the top of her breastbone was lightly hidden by a coloured feather in honour of the profession of her host. Red-gold clip-on earrings completed her attire.

When George had told him about the plan for the unveiling, Nicolas has insisted he ask the Swedish diplomat Erik Magnus Staël von Holstein. Nicolas had described to his friend the Swede's interest in the animal kingdom as an admirer of his compatriot the great naturalist and explorer Carolus Linnaeus, who had proposed a system for classifying and naming all species. The charming and good-looking Staël, after five years of negotiation through their common friend Marie Antoinette, had finally wed the formidable Germaine earlier in the year. She was the young daughter of Necker, the immensely wealthy Swiss minister of finance at the Versailles court. Staël had been promoted to an ambassador as part of a negotiation with the Swedish crown, and France had given a Caribbean island to Sweden, although a smaller one than the king had hoped for.[21]

"Seriously, a French island for the marriage of the daughter of a minister?" George had exclaimed.

"Indeed, but you must know, while Sweden has many more islands than France, they tend to be inhospitable and swarming with mosquitoes," Nicolas had explained. "Staël was fascinated with Germaine, but she also solved the financial predicaments of diminished family wealth being combined with a taste for the gaming table. Thus, the intervention of the kings of Sweden and France concluded this oddest of deals, sealing the wedding between the granddaughter of a protestant pastor from Geneva and an impoverished Swedish nobleman. Germaine, on the other hand, probably saw him as a man whose conduct is perfectly correct, incapable of behaving stupidly, with a focussed interest in botany, but ultimately sterile and inert for her grand aspirations." Nicolas had acidly speculated that he would likely not make her unhappy, for the simple reason that he could not contribute to her happiness, and not because he could trouble it.[22]

He concluded, "Given her hurricane of a temperament, it would not surprise me that her children will come from many fathers, but he will be so bound to her fortune that he will oblige by recognising them all."

Nicolas had been amongst the first guests arriving, a mark

21 In 1877, Sweden sold the island back to France.

22 Herold, 1958.

of honour for his friend given that his standing would have warranted arriving amongst the last. When Staël's carriage arrived, Nicolas introduced him, lauding George's sensibility to natural philosophy and his deep experience acquired in his profession. The ambassador expressed his appreciation for the invitation to this unusual zebra unveiling and mentioned that George's reputation extended to Stockholm.

George couldn't help but blush—astonished that he might be known so far north.

"Monsieur du Paon, what is your opinion of Linnaeus's project to deconstruct nature into distinct categories?" Staël asked. "Linnaeus aims to unveil a deeper connection between the parts of nature, and to thereby separate them into his defined groups. Yet, at the same time, this approach fails to explain why an *Equus africanus asinus* could be domesticated and an *Equus zebra* not!"

"Your Excellency, it is a great honour that you grace our unveiling with your presence. Nicolas had told me that you are a tremendous scholar of nature. I agree with you that deconstructing nature as Linnaeus proposes helps us greatly in recognising what we are looking at, but it appears to take us further away from understanding how nature functions," countered George.

"Indeed, it does not help much for this purpose," Staël agreed with a vigorous nod, looking around the courtyard.

He went on to describe how his colleague representing Sweden at the court of Saxen-Weimar had drawn his attention to the writings of a certain von Goethe, who was said to be working on a description of the metamorphosis of plants that promised to go well beyond Linnaeus. In it, he addressed how plants had common traits rather than reducing nature to its components.

Straightening himself, Nicolas gently closed the conversation, and George appreciated his efforts to liberate him for his other guests. "Fascinating. We must all be sure to investigate this von Goethe," Nicolas said. "Perhaps he can shed light on the debate at the Versailles court on the connection between donkeys and zebras. Or perhaps George's work will provide the answer!"

They were soon drowned out by the sounds of the first sonata of Joseph Bologne, a favourite composer of George's that he had often had the opportunity to hear. Of African descent, born in Guadeloupe, Bologne struck an unusual figure in Paris and had become widely known for his music. A polymath, he was feared by many as a skilled fencer and well known as an abolitionist diplomat. He was also in great demand as an anonymous lover, following the title of his eponymous opera. For George, Bologne's music captured the ambiguous lightheartedness of the time.

All the guests had now arrived and taken their place in the unrecognisable atelier. As the sonata ended, and after a few words from George, the zebra was ceremonially unveiled as Jeanne pulled back the silk cover with a fell swoop. Just as gracefully as she had covered it, she now disrobed it for all to see, taking a few steps backwards as she did.

The audience contentedly murmured at the sight of the pattern of the animal. George could assume that most had heard about zebras, but by the surprised looks upon their faces, it was clear that they had never observed one directly. Champagne coupes were raised to the result. Du Paon's atelier was praised and celebrated by all. Despite the momentary elation, after a quick stroll around the beast, the guests resumed their conversations. Bologne's successive sonatas appeared to convey playful motion even to the watchful and stilted animals in the cupboards. George overcame his natural social reticence to mix with the guests, resigned to float with the flow of their words, when he really wanted to embrace Jeanne and Gaston.

Jeanne had no such social qualms, and George observed with some satisfaction that she very much held her own in conversations with groups of guests who seemed under her charm, prodded by the praise he had expressed before she pulled the zebra's veil. Finally finding a moment to congratulate her, she told him that she could not help but feel a twinge of regret, as she contrasted the energy and dedication that had gone into every detail with the feather-light appreciation expressed through the crowd's enthusiasm. George emphasised that he was very proud of her—and of Gaston—and that she should be confident in her own judgement of her work.

"It is the way of the world that praise will be expressed in conversations that we will never witness, and we will also notice through continued commissions for the atelier," he hurriedly added before being swept away by Nicolas. He noticed from the corner of his eye that Gaston had fetched another case of champagne destined to join the row of empty bottles. The room had within it the spark and the excitement emanating from a successful event. One which had fed the senses of his guests. It seemed that the audience had not, as he had initially surmised, dismissed the unveiling. Condorcet himself exuded enthusiasm about the zebra and was most impressed with how it evoked the raw force of nature and a sense of its wildness.

"The black-and-white contrast of the animal appeared to echo the duality of the natural and the human orders," he said with marked excitement in his voice. "Let us present the zebra at the Académie des sciences before it needs to be shipped back to London. I realise this is not an obvious enterprise, as you know attendance is strictly off-limits for non-members, but it is entirely out of the question that you would not be present."

"You think?" George set the glass of wine he had been carrying on the adorned worktable and steadied himself. Nicolas's suggestion was not a possibility he had considered.

"Yes! And a presentation would also further expose the fact that the British royal zebra was in Paris, but with today's noisy success, that appears to be the smaller issue. Again, not an obvious enterprise, but achievable."

The idea was further hobbled by George's insistence that Jeanne, as the main author of the work, should imperatively attend. George knew, of course, that women were entirely prohibited from even entering the Académie.

"This is an easy enough problem to solve," George countered to Nicolas's reference to the rules of the Académie, "as Jeanne could simply join dressed as a man. If the Chevalier d'Éon—a veteran general who took to dressing as a woman from the age of forty-nine—could be an accepted and prominent member of society, then surely a young female artisan could attend a lecture disguised as a male student or assistant?"

Condorcet conceded on gender, titillated in passing at the thought of manipulating the identity of George's servant.

"Let's go over and speak with Buffon, but not a word about Jeanne," Nicolas sternly admonished his friend.

A short conversation was sufficient for Nicolas to convince Buffon for them to jointly approach the president of the Académie about exceptionally allowing George to attend, accompanied by one of his brilliant assistants.

George could not wait to inform Jeanne—she would be deeply curious, albeit a tad insecure, as was her nature.

•

The societal superficiality at the unveiling of the zebra had left George longing for human closeness. The guests took their leave, but Mathilde Joussereau stayed on, starting the rest of the evening with a celebratory dinner with George in his apartments that he did not need to insist upon—Mathilde smiled brightly at the invitation, clearly pleased to have the honour and the intimacy. Her sustained attention for George at the Café de Foy had led to an arrangement that he believed satisfied them both. Being occasional lovers allowed them to keep their closest nature to themselves, while indulging in the occasional rush of physical pleasure. They had discovered that they were both skilful lovers, sharing a temperament for skirting boundaries.

Jacques had prepared a fire, and the bearskin rug—from a commission that had been left uncollected when its owner perished in a foolhardy duel—was an apt stage.

Mathilde swiftly stripped him of his boots, ribbons, coat, breeches, shirt, and underdrawers. They stood for a moment side by side, interrogating their reflection in the large mirror. An elegant woman in a formal green dress, contented that she had been invited by this naked man. George tightened his stomach imperceptibly, offsetting the slackening of his abdomen from indulgent evenings. He noticed that his musculature from the regular handling of heavy loads continued to please Mathilde, which she acknowledged with an approving smile in the direction of his rising excitement.

He removed her ear clips, appreciating their lack of penetration of the flesh of the lobes, carefully laid the feather on a side table, and dropped the green taffeta onto the fur. Several more technical grips released Mathilde from the restraint of the white silk busk by pulling out the long red laces on her backside. The corset was a traditional one, flattening her bosom, without the fashionable orbs that would have lifted her roundness. A remaining whiff of powder and rose scent bore witness to his anticipation of the twin unveilings of the day—and hers, it seemed, as well.

With his thumbs, George proceeded to gently massage the red marks of the corset on her loins, the lengthy stripes from the whale bones, punctuated by a row of dots where the laces had entered the grommets.

Relieved to be liberated of her fashion harness, Mathilde stretched contentedly, abandoning herself to his caresses. Ever the entertaining hostess, she whispered a reference to the Marquis de Sade that he had read to her in the afterlight of another tryst.

"My body," she murmured, "is the church where Nature asks to be reverenced."

Suppressing a fleeting vision of Violette's cheekbone, George fled to the hem of Mathilde's long satin stockings. He dedicated himself to her pleasure, completing a journey through the senses, through sight, sound, and smell, to taste and touch.[23] Bringing Mathilde to the brink of divine bliss, pinching her rosebuds to the verge of pain, George himself was transported by Mathilde's surrender.

---

23 Sight, sound, smell, taste, and touch is the order of the medieval senses, as represented, for example, in the six tapestries of *La Dame à la licorne*, leading to an enigmatic sixth sense.

5

The Académie

The Académie royale des sciences, created by Colbert in 1699, consisted of seventy members chosen for life, amongst them Buffon and Condorcet. Well before becoming America's envoy to France, Benjamin Franklin had been an associate member since 1772, in recognition of his groundbreaking work on electricity—most notably the invention of the lightning rod, an innovation that had changed the safety of shipping and saved churches like Paris's Notre Dame Cathedral from fiery destruction. The debate about zebra domestication had acquired such prominence, along with the rumour of the exceptional presence of the British royal zebra on French soil, that Buffon and Condorcet had little difficulty in convincing the president to insert a viewing in a scheduled session the following week.

George and Jeanne were not about to let the zebra out of their sight and rode with it in the cart to the Louvre, where the Académie had its seat in the half-finished construction of the cavernous palace. The building had lost its purpose when Louis XIV moved the court from Paris to Versailles, and now hosted various institutions and initiatives in its vast spaces. Thanks to the innovative construction of the zebra's internal scaffolding, the creature had remained relatively light and manoeuvrable. A discreet chariot had been borrowed from Maître Fingret on the Place Royale where George—as was common in Paris—rented the furniture of his apartment.[24] The coarse wooden cart with its large rear wheels was drawn by two ruddy horses and covered by an unmarked linen batch, hiding its odd freight from view. It had halted under one of the extended archways leading into the main courtyard of the Louvre. Four footmen were waiting to help carry the precious load up the stairs into the rooms of the Académie.

George stood to the side and watched as the zebra was eased out of the chariot and gently lowered onto the granite cobblestones. The orange fabric of the lackeys' uniforms contrasted with the black and white of the zebra, which was soon shrouded by a heavy linen cloth. Two sturdy purple linen straps were slung under the zebra's belly and tied to a long wooden pole, which they shouldered to carry the beast up the stairs.

The hall granted to the scientists had previously been part of the king's apartments in the Louvre. It had a magnificent

---

24 Dumas, 1860, ch. 14.

painted ceiling from the period of Henri II and high crossbar windows on each of the long sides. The walls were covered with Abbeville damask in front of which stood eighteen busts of scientists along with a sprinkling of princes. Above the chimney at the end of the hall hung a large painting by Antoine Coypel depicting a regal Minerva holding an oval portrait of the king, with a skeleton behind her chair and a globe in front. The adjacent room where they had temporarily deposited the zebra had previously been the king's bedroom.[25]

George waited in this former royal bedroom until Nicolas entered to invite him in. Buffon and Condorcet were the joint hosts for this part of the gathering. With an undulating motion of his hand, the elderly botanist gestured George towards a seat on a richly decorated but rather hard bench situated under the windows. From there George observed, with some amusement, how Jeanne was unrecognisable in an elegant light yellow coat, her abundant dark hair hidden from sight under a male wig. She pushed in the zebra. The animal was perched for this purpose on a plank equipped with small wooden wheels covered with caoutchouc, a new material from the hevea tree that had been brought back in 1736 by one of the members, Charles-Marie de La Condamine, during an expedition to South America. The elastic material eased the creaking of the makeshift carriage on the parquet flooring.

The scientists were seated on tiered benches along the length of the room. Maurepas, Chappe d'Auteroche, d'Abbadie,

25 Babeau, 1895.

Grandjean de Fouchy, du Hamel de Monceau, and the physicists Ampère, Coulomb, and Laplace were all prominently seated in the first row.

When the animal was unveiled, murmurs spread around the room. George could assume that most of the attendees had only ever seen prints of a zebra, and never one even tangential to life. Its stark black-and-white contrast appeared to reproach the baroque ornaments of the room. A cacophony erupted, suspending the Académie's strict protocol, which Nicolas had described to George in advance in elaborate detail. Rising from their seats, members huddled around the object, unceremoniously pushing away George and Jeanne, leaving them to idle by a large and generously gilded table surmounted by a portrait of Blaise Pascal gazing disapprovingly.

After fifteen minutes of bustle, Buffon managed to coax the members back into their chairs, launching a debate on the nature of nature. George was left confused by what he heard: a philosophical joust highjacked by emotion into a political crusade.

Buffon opened the session by recounting the failed experiments both at Versailles and Windsor to domesticate the zebra. "They tried everything. Cavalry officers confidently strode towards the zebra only to be unceremoniously thrown off, and one was so viciously bitten that he lost the function of his hand. The head farmer of the royal estates was kicked by the stubborn beast. Mules were brought to create a bit of herd, but they simply ignored each other."

Jeanne turned to George with a restrained, knowing smile, recalling his description of the attempt to paint an ass with stripes to seduce the zebra. Her back straightened with pride at her success in grasping nature's fury, with a slight shudder of anticipation at the judgement of the illustrious gathering.

A few members objected that surely it had been poorly done and that their own centennial chivalrous heritages would be no match for the beast. Once those voices had exhausted themselves, the discussion turned first to nature, then to causality.

Lavoisier asked whether life could really be described in finite terms or whether we might here be faced with proof that an element existed that was both undoubtedly true but unprovable.[26] He carefully noted that his argument pertained to the living part of nature, not to the physical reality. A brouhaha ensued, with members calling such views a threat to the essence of the Enlightenment, portending a return to an era of revealed truth as the source of authority, or even worse, a universal subjectivism where anyone's opinion might carry weight.

Then Lazzaro Spallanzani, a correspondent member from the University of Pavia who was temporarily residing in Paris, went on an extended argument about the origins of the mechanisation of our worldview.[27] Spallanzani had a tall forehead framed by a deeply receding hairline, a slightly hunched stance, pale skin, and a high-pitched voice; he looked the part of the scholar. He was always reaching for the long wave of history, rather than being seduced by the argument of the day. Spallanzani was a biologist and a priest, with an outstanding

---

26 A prelude to Gödel's theorem that 145 years later would be the death knell of the Enlightenment dream that a complete mathematical representation could be found.

27 Dijksterhuis, 1950.

command of Greek. His contributions to the idea of spontaneous generation, whereby life evolved from inanimate matter, had made him famous. The first artificial insemination of a dog added to his reputation. His control of French was excellent, although buoyed by a heavy Italian accent, which modulated the melody of his speech. He relished in portraying history as a joust of competing ideas.

•

Several hours later, Jeanne and George carried the zebra back to the cart with the assistance of the lackeys of the Académie. The cool autumn drizzle hit them as soon as they emerged through the archway from the broad staircase back into the courtyard of the Louvre. The hall had been poorly ventilated and had grown increasingly rancid from the scalding arguments of the assembled scientists, several of whom had adopted the American habit of smoking tobacco in a pipe. George was nursing a mild headache while Jeanne appeared distracted.

Soon they were back in the rue des Saints-Pères, welcomed back by Gaston's familiar whistling in a distant room. They spent a short time reminiscing about the afternoon, an odd conversation as Jeanne was still dressed as a man. George realised that he spoke to her in a slightly different tone, marginally more polemic, substituting opinions where observations might have been more appropriate. He could not decide whether it was attributable to the physical metamorphosis of Jeanne or to the influence of the intense dialectic squabbles that he had witnessed earlier.

Looking distractedly at the shining, rain-soaked tin roofs beyond the window, Jeanne murmured, "Such learned men grandly quoting authors I have never even heard of, counter-quoting each with pride in their voices, over and over. But then suddenly seeming small and self-centred: 'Everybody is convinced of this or that . . .' or 'any priest will tell you . . .' One moment they are imposing scientists, the next one they are just ordinary men."

"Indeed. It was as if in a wild garden where too many plants compete for attention," explained George, "then the arguments form a décor within which for a time a single voice sounds, until it, too, withers and is absorbed back into the swirling tide of opinions. It is how men are. Sometimes scientists, and always just men."

Turning her gaze from the window, Jeanne gave George a look of appreciation. "I am very grateful for your insistence that I attend the meeting," she told him gently, a pained look nonetheless in her eye. "It is a world completely foreign to me. Like looking through a window into an unknown part of society. Strange. I thought I wouldn't understand a word, and then . . ."

George saw that the experience had left her confused about her own capacities and that it had further underscored how sharply her future would be constrained by her origins and her gender, notwithstanding his own efforts at promoting her.

After Jeanne had retired to her room, George locked the front gate by lowering the heavy iron rod into the brackets on each door. He twice checked that he had indeed turned the large key activating the lock of the door to the atelier. Then he turned and climbed the stairs to his apartment. Jacques had prepared a fire and, after swapping his formal clothes for a more comfortable housecoat, he settled at the small table next to the hearth. In addition to several paintings that covered the walls and the small portrait of Violette he ritually glanced towards, it was the one item of furniture that he did not rent. It had been handed down to him from the house of his parents: a simple oak table. He opened the large binder covered in the coarse leather of an elephant, an item that had been gifted to him by Buffon after a small favour, the nature of which he could not recall. George proceeded to document the conversations that he and Jeanne had witnessed.

He attempted to reproduce the essence of Spallanzani's very extended exposé.

"We cannot make sense of the zebra we have in front of us today," he had started, "because centuries of competition amongst ideas have formed and constrained the thoughts our minds are capable of formulating. Plato taught us to value the ideal over matter and Democritus that this matter was built of simple components."

Pythagoras, Spallanzani opined, had laid the foundation for our mechanical-reductionist view of the world, which has held sway until this day, taking central stage in the Enlightenment. Pythagoras had articulated the belief that all of reality could be represented through numbers, in abstract and pure mathematics. Aristotle had echoed this, stating, "Things are numbers." In his quest for pure knowledge, Pythagoras affirmed an ascetic approach to reality, one valuing immateriality above all, delivering a cleansing of the soul and liberation from the constraints of the senses, the confusion of the material world, and the whirlwind vagaries of nature.

Then Democritus's atomism had laid the foundation for materialism, as it assumed that everything happened through direct causality on those atoms. The idea of direct causality stuck, although what constitutes atoms has evolved. Titus Lucretius Carus nailed the concept of atomism for all eternity through his epic philosophical poem *On the Nature of Things*.

Although Plato added his own views, they echoed Pythagoras's belief in the primacy of pure mathematics at the expense of empirical knowledge, which Plato considered feminine and inferior. The sensory world was a mere projection of the real world—it was second-rate. The real world could only be accessed through the mind, not through the senses.

George was interrupted from his recollections by a loud noise from the floor above him and laid down his plume. Silence. He imagined his upstairs neighbour had perhaps tripped or overturned a chair. His mind returned to Plato and his curious views on what is real. A naturalised zebra is surely not a projection of the real world. Quite the opposite, it is a way to access what is real in the world, to grasp the forces of nature behind the scenes. Or perhaps Plato was right after all, and both a real zebra and stuffed one are just projections that we use to gain knowledge of the abstract. George dipped his plume in the deep-purple ink that he had mixed for his use and returned to capturing his memory of the debates at the Académie.

Spallanzani had continued to describe Plato's dialogue where Timaios, the good demiurge, has sculpted a physical world from a chaotic state of matter, following an eternal set of ideas. Raising his voice for effect, curling a raised finger in the air, he proclaimed, "To create a three-dimensional world, by mathematical necessity he needed two polarities, not just one: earth and fire on the one hand, water and air on the other. Plato's atomism was not the same as Democritus's, based on divisible mathematical shapes, but it was a reductionist view, nevertheless. Aristotle might have provided an escape from the concept that pure ideas were more real than the messy reality that our senses reveal. Aristotle was undoubtedly genuinely interested in the natural world, and his writings demonstrate the curiosity of a true empiricist. He developed real machines, like the water organ, and an analysis of hearing as a cochlea-shaped, air-filled cavity in the head."

Spallanzani had paused for breath, looking down at his feet for an uncomfortably long silence. Jeanne had appeared thrilled by the theatrics as much as by the concepts. She later told George that the words floated in and out of her mind, leaving ridges and furrows that she was convinced would divulge their meaning over the years. He had been amused when she asked him whether he had ever met these gentlemen Aristotle and Plato, and what they were like.

Spallanzani had concluded: "Aristotle contrasted with Plato, who considered the physical world beneath his dignity and interest. So why did Aristotle make so relatively little lasting progress? At least from the modern perspective of the eighteenth century, the problem was that the intellectual culture in which he operated was not conducive to a rich theory based on painstaking empirical research. Instead, a relatively superficial theory was cobbled together based on the four elements that were easily intelligible to the senses. And even that work was dismissed by Plutarch as mere distractions from the noble work of pure geometry. As a result, the Greeks' mastery of the physical sciences never matched the sophistication they reached in geometry.

"They debated mathematics in natural language. Their lack of a formal language of equations led them to neglect algebra. But algebra was more useful to explore problems in the world than those in the mind, so they lost the chance to build on the legacy of Babylonia and left it to the Arabs many centuries later to pick up the baton. The Greeks favoured pure geometry in the mind at the expense of practical algebra in the world. In any case, Aristotle's passion for at least engaging with reality as it is, rather than as we would like it to be, was lost to European culture until the Arabs reintroduced it in Europe in twelfth-century Toledo."

A knock on the door announced Jacques, who had prepared an infusion of verbena that soothed George's unruly stomach in the evening. Sleep during the previous night in Mathilde's company had been scarce and restless. While briefly relishing the memory, he knocked over the ink pot with his elbow.

"Jacques!" he shouted in frustration.

"Yes, how may—" Interrupting himself upon seeing the purple spill dripping over the edge of the table and onto the floor, Jacques quickly ran for a bucket and a rag.

"Thank you, thank you. I am so clumsy. It's probably too late."

The ink's penetrating power quickly stained the cracks in the oak of the parquet floor, with a shape reminiscent of a bird's feather. Suppressing a curse at the lasting mark, he dove back into his recollection of the afternoon at the Académie.

George had been startled when Spallanzani, a part-time abbot who regularly held mass in his local church in Pavia, laid bare the contribution of early Christianity and how deeply it was rooted in Greek thought. Perhaps under the influence of the illustrious halls of the Louvre and his colleagues, the mind of the scientist dominated the convictions of the clergyman. The rise of Christianity had been a new challenge for scientific thinking. Although some of the church fathers, like Augustinus, were tolerant of the natural sciences, others were not.

Basil of Caesarea wrote, in the influential *Hexaemeron*, that nature should be studied exclusively as the creation of God. Platonic thinking emerged as the dominant influence, degrading the physical world to secondary status for many centuries. This cemented the dominance of the ideal pure world over the messy material one. And the ideal pure world was one of direct causality, reducing the individual's perspective to a mechanistic model of reality. Not because it had to be, but because the mathematics that were available could not deal with anything more complex. This in turn defined religion, culture, and philosophy. As a result, Spallanzani had declaimed, with Italian pathos, that "we have no way of really understanding the life that inhabited our zebra here—and why it was not tameable like an ass."

At this point, Spallanzani was interrupted by another speaker, whom George had not been able to identify. This man had stood up, exalted. To George's surprise he was much more rotund that he expected, causing him to briefly wonder whether the earthly pleasures of food and those of the mind were compatible.

"You fail to do justice to the Arab cultures' role in saving our civilisation from the tight embrace of an overbearing church." The unknown man pontificated with the injured tone of one who was not assured of his place in this tight elite and rendered impatient by the erudition on display and desiring to counter with an exhibition of equal knowledge.

This was an unfair and odd altercation, as Spallanzani had gone further in challenging the role of the church than was useful and perhaps wise. Nevertheless, the speaker responded by further celebrating the role of the Arabs and stated that the various Islamic civilisations deserve complete credit for preserving and reintroducing Greek thought in Europe. George was aware of this and indeed had collected a small library of Arab philosophers over the years. His interest, of course, extended to the millenary embalming tradition in Egypt.

In the areas of astronomy and algebra, the Arabs also contributed new work but built mainly on an extraordinary Hellenic foundation. Mathematician Al-Huwârizmî, also known as Algoritmi, Aristotelian al-Kindî, the astronomers Tâbit Qurra, al-Fargânî, al Battânî, and Ibn al-Haytam—and of course the giant of them all, Averroës. He continued to emphasise that today's members of society owed perhaps the greatest debt to Averroës's absolute worship of Aristotle, along with his resolute distancing of science and religion. But it was—and George found this to be an interesting point—the countless translators who did the difficult job of creating new texts in various European languages that not only had forgotten the ideas, but often no longer had the vocabulary to express them in. This work happened mostly in Spain, centred in Toledo, where the knowledge of Arabic remained widespread. The converted Jew Johannes Hispalensis, the Christian Robert of Chester, and Gerard of Cremona or the Jew Savasorda all dedicated their lives to reintroducing the lost manuscripts.

George had furiously made notes during the meeting, allowing him to transcribe the events into his diary.

"Indeed, *cher confrère*, your historic learning serves you well, and you are a true scholar." Spallanzani manoeuvred deftly between erudite discourse and the management of the dented ego. "You are of course right, the Arabs brought back Greek thought in the twelfth century, most crucially Aristotle." Spallanzani proceeded to describe the tortuous pathway from the Greek philosophers' flight away from the messiness of daily life into a pure world of ideas. Remarkably, this conviction had been passed down through centuries, and had, in its wake, created two new world religions, and ultimately determined how the Académie reacted to a stuffed zebra.

"Thomas of Aquino," Spallanzani had continued, "pulls off an amazing feat, by postulating the necessary consistency of the *sacra doctrina* and rational thought. People should think freely and advance science because it will necessarily be consistent with the umbrella of religious thought. Contradiction is unthinkable, as religious thought is perfect."

Spallanzani expounded on how rational thought, like contemplation, is a different path that will lead to God. And thus, science suddenly acquired a legitimate place in Christian society, although a tentative one as it was constrained by an appeal to the church authorities on the one hand, and an excessive awe of Aristotle on the other hand—partly fuelled by his biggest fan Averroës. There were a few early exceptions in the thirteenth century to this sterile compliance, such as the Englishman Roger Bacon and Pierre Pelerin de Maricourt, unusually not a monk but a nobleman and a rare experimental scientist, whom George knew many still admired for his work on magnetism.

Clearly perceiving restlessness amongst his audience—George himself was made anxious by it—Spallanzani sought to regain attention and conclude, his Italian accent seemingly deepening through the sustained effort. "Why, my learned friends, have I gone to such lengths to explore the radices of our inability to grasp the nature of what is in front of us? Indeed, what is the nature of the zebra that Signor du Paon has somewhat reincarnated? I have argued we struggle because we have inherited a narrow view of causality from Democritus and a disdain for reality from Plato. When they did not end up burnt at the stake or in prison, our predecessors found a way out of this dilemma that is more meaningful than it appears at first blush: the occult. The occult was understood in the twelfth century and inadvertently celebrated by Molière!"

Spallanzani paused for dramatic effect, as the audience grumbled.

"Not wild beliefs such as that the echinus fish has the capacity to hold back ships, the term *occult* is used to describe properties that are not attributable to matter, such as why opium leads to sleep, as Molière asks in *Le Malade imaginaire* and Thomas Diafoirus replies, 'Because it has dormitive power that leads to sleep.' And why we experience an octave—or indeed that a zebra is untameable. All these things can be justly described as occult properties. They are real and observable properties, but we can identify no cause to derive them from. Is an atom of water wet? Why is a zebra wild? The properties appear to emerge somehow—I propose we refer to those properties that exist exclusively at the highest observable level as occult. Others, such as Descartes or indeed our esteemed colleague Laplace, introduced demons to fill gaps in the fabric of scientific explanation.[28] However, these still have a place in time and space. Our idea of the occult is more ethereal. Then came Newton."

George recalled how Spallanzani had let the name of the great man fill the room, looking intently at each member of the audience, his palms raised as if solemnly blessing the audience through the invocation of Newton.

"Newton wrestled with the basic forces of motion, capturing them in a set of axioms. You will be familiar with his second axiom: '*Mutationem motus proportionalem esse vi motrici*

---

28 Canales, 2020.

impressae, et fieri secundum lineam rectam qua vis illa imprimitur.'[29] As revolutionary as that was just over a century ago, we can see that Newton remained less than clear on the relationship between *quantitas absolutas*, *quantitas acceleratrix*, and *quantitas motrix*, as the three units of the central force of motion. He laid out the principles on which mechanics are based today. Pascal had done something similar with hydrostatics, yet while most of the ideas were present before Newton, it was a chaotic heap of inconsistent and not-always-coherent intuitive concepts. Forces had initially been seen as causing motion and were then described as its consequence."

In order to expand his knowledge of the natural sciences, George had acquired, over the years, a basic knowledge of the teachings of the great men. Diderot's monumental *Encyclopédie* was accessible in the reading room he frequented in the Palais-Royal, and it provided accessible and compact summaries. Newton's ideas embodied the culmination of centuries of development. An enormous achievement, but one focussed on the narrowest of questions, namely the motion of inanimate objects in an idealised space. It didn't come as a surprise to George that the first spectacular application was for the motion of stellar objects, whizzing around in a cold void, devoid of any of the intricacies of life's forces or indeed of the spirit. The laws of gravitation perfectly describe how the attraction of objects to each other accurately predicted their motion in space with impressive

29 The alteration of motion is ever proportional to the motive force impressed; and is made in the direction of the right line in which that force is impressed.

precision. George had marvelled at the simple relation for the attraction between two masses as inversely proportional to their distance, a law that held across unimaginably large distances. In this, George believed that Newton surpassed all his predecessors, from Pythagoras to Kepler. Newton appeared to have fallen back to the scholastic idea of action at a distance, without the intervention of a connecting medium. Mechanics without a mechanism. His critics saw him reverting to Aristotelean causality. Why does a ball fall to earth? Because of the mutual attraction between them, according to Newton; because the ball wants to go home, according to Aristotle.

With a touch of drama, Spallanzani concluded: "Dangerously similar, my learned friends, only with a mathematical sleight of hand!"

And although Newton's mathematics had more predictive power for the motion of stellar bodies, he was a deeply pious man and saw the hand of God in the creation of these relationships and endowing matter with the properties he observed. He did not feel the need for deeper explanations, as divine design sufficed.

Spallanzani continued: "Newton vehemently rejected the occult—which we discussed earlier—as a possible explanation for the kind of things that appear to emerge without direct causality. The difference between Aristotle and Newton is not as big as it seems. Both describe empirical laws, without an underlying explanation, holding out the hope that one could be found. Both have reserved a place for God, but Newton's God is one at rest after the creation, not needing much involvement in the daily running of the world. In fact, our colleague Laplace brilliantly read to us his thoughts on the planetary motions only thirteen years ago in these very halls. Only last year, he resolved the mathematical grounds for the great Jupiter-Saturn inequality. God appears ever more retired, with his universe running like an elaborate clock. In the process, we have convinced ourselves that these laws of mechanics are the laws of nature. That all phenomena can be described with simple linear or differential equations, that God was only present at the beginning, and that the occult does not exist."

"Cher Marchese de Laplace, can you explain why this zebra could not be tamed?" Spallanzani had interrupted his monologue to pull in the audience but was met with a pregnant silence. The learned assembly had for a moment suspended their trigger-ready opinions to hear where he was headed.

Then the marquis sternly corrected him. "Kinetics, not mechanics. The term was poorly chosen. What Newton had formulated was a science of kinetics describing motion; mechanics implies all sorts of things about the world that are not warranted. He also did so in purely functional terms, taking away the teleology. That was not a historical necessity, as for example the former member Maupertuis formulated the principle of least action almost forty years ago. That was a remarkable insight, which he saw as the artistic elegance of the hand of God, always finding the path in the world that minimises work. Not for Newton, who was interested in describing, rather than explaining. And he did so in mathematical terms."

Ignoring the interruption, Spallanzani finally started his conclusion. "This, gentlemen," he said grandly, flinging his arms wide, "largely fixed our worldview. Which brings us back to our zebra. Clearly, we can't explain why it can't be domesticated, let alone why it is alive. At least when it was alive. It is not excluded that our mathematics will evolve to help answer these questions, but it is also not a given that we will ever have a mathematics of the occult. One that describes emergent properties, rather than those intimately associated with matter. The greater danger is that we settle on a mechanistic, or more precisely a kinetic view of the world—which may well remain with us for centuries and blind us to its richness.

"That, my friends, is the reason this work is important, as indeed other works of art can be, to give us an understanding of the world beyond the constraints we inherited from Newton's closure of centuries of intellectual wanderings."

Then Beaubourg spoke. George had recognised him from Madame du Barry's table at the Café de Foy. Beaubourg was known to speak little and to be a keen observer. Unusually in this assembly of scientists, he was an accomplished painter who specialised in detailed and refined studies of flowers, or preferably of details of flowers. His work was reminiscent of the great naturalists of the seventeenth century such as the Dutch painter Otto Marseus van Schriek, whose dense undergrowth depictions teemed with dragonflies, mushrooms, and snakes rendered in vivid detail.

Beaubourg proceeded to describe how the wildness of the zebra was visible for all to see if one chose to observe it at length in the present specimen. And that this approximated the organising force of nature itself. He explained that this devilish object unveiled that force and made it accessible to those who understood it.

"This zebra is a dangerous weapon!" he proclaimed. He was assaulted by his colleagues, who accused him of being a Kantian or a modern Goethean, which was considered an even worse Germanic slander.

George remembered his surprise at becoming a subject in the debate when Laplace injected, "Gentlemen, gentlemen, calm down. What we were looking at is the interpretation of Monsieur de Paon of a zebra, not even at the zebra itself!"

Undeterred, Beaubourg had proposed that his colleagues consider merely the possibility that he was right. And that if this knowledge were available to British scientists with their empirical tradition, that this would provide English science with a great advantage over France. How strongly would they wager on him being wrong? He was soon drowned out by members, their lips sharply pursed just before speaking, to give their words greater momentum, launching accusations of absurdity, of fearmongering, sensationalism, and unscientific thinking. The members had disagreed whether the zebra was a work of art—a revelation or the product of scientific dedication.

They did agree on one thing—that it was French skill and tradition that made it possible to reveal the nature of the wild animal. Nowhere else in Europe cou ld this have been accomplished.

Condorcet had sat quietly in the front row. George recalled how his brow had furrowed, and he had apologised later, feeling sorry that his friend together with his transvestite collaborator should witness this degree of confusion and that the impact of their work was sacrificed for diminutive oratory victory laps.

George had found the discussion on the source of the materialistic spirit of the day interesting. History had driven humanity to the point of reducing reality into simple causality. But was the occult the only way of describing how phenomena could avoid being reduced to their constituent elements? Would mathematics, as Spallanzani had wondered, evolve to enlighten, and include the occult? And did the zebra indeed betray those occult properties, making it the powerful cultural weapon that Beaubourg was surmising?

George closed the elephant binder.

6

Chloë d'Avigny

Control over the Palais Anti-Royal, as it was sometimes called, eluded the authorities.[30] It remained beyond the reach of the royal police; its entrance guarded by Swiss mercenaries in the pay of Orléans. "Now that you are a shopkeeper, Duke, we shall only see you on Sundays," Louis XVI had quipped to his real estate developer brother. An eruption of ideas, sin, fantasies, and art was the result. George and Nicolas had debated how this cauldron might someday spin out of

---

30 The Palais-Royal was to become the cradle of a developing revolutionary fervour in the lead up to 1789. After the revolution had absorbed the ideas from the cauldron and beheaded the rich clientele of the courtisanes, a "petition from the twenty-one hundred girls of the Palais-Royal to the National Assembly" would be sent to the new authorities to secure their right to work. A later catalogue describing the girls was a desperate attempt to set back the clock to the golden years of the eighties. In addition to their rate, Chouchou, Bienfaite, Zaïre, Coquine, and Boutonderose listed their size, hair colour, conversation, voluptuousness, or gait, as well as any distinctive skills.

control and a veritable revolution might erupt from the garden. It was as if this little society was frantically dancing, crying for help to dislodge itself from its paralysis.

Through the wide window at the beginning of the long columned gallery, George could see a row of girls on a long bench against the mirror-covered wall. Bunches of flowers were spread across from them, dominated by the yellows and oranges of the late season. Spring was on the opposite side: bright red dresses, white bonnets, ribbons in all colours, each trying to attract attention over their competitors, armed with a more effusive flowery perfume. In passing, George had smiled at the calculating shrewdness of the owner, who had sat the prettiest faces closest to the window.

As George emerged from the colonnade to make his way to the Café de Foy in the opposite gallery, he glanced at the first-floor windows of Chloë d'Avigny's apartment, in the faint expectation to perhaps catch a view of Nicolas's profile against the candlelight.

As often, Nicolas and George had agreed to meet after dinner at the Café de Foy and proceed from there to one of the houses they frequented with some regularity. Mathilde smiled when she saw George enter through the doorway that gave access to the stairs from the Galerie Montpensier—Nicolas's earlier presence had apparently foreboded his imminent arrival.

George joined his friend at the table in the southernmost corner, looking over the square patterns of the barren branches in the garden of the Palais. They briefly alluded to the previous day's presentation at the Académie, but still intellectually recovering, George quickly moved on to more mundane topics, asking with a dose of mischief, "Is Chloë anything like Mademoiselle de Boubers?"

"I would rather not be reminded of that unfortunate episode. Inspecteur Lenoir saved me from ignominy. And Amélie has the grace to forgive me for seducing her young niece. In my defence, I was saving her from being condemned to watch the grass grow in Fontenay, away from my admittedly overzealous passions," rebutted Nicolas, with a slight grimace.

George recalled with some bitterness the episode where his enlightened friend had rather unfortunately become enthralled by the eighteen-year-old niece of his friend Madame Amélie Suard. Inexplicably for someone whose mood could darken from witnessing a superficial conversation or an argument's mere inconsistency, he had been bewitched by the promise and freshness of youth, clouding the limits of her intellect with a benign veil.

"And did you see her yesterday?"

"Indeed—and, as usual, Chloë's maid kept me waiting for a long time in the small antechamber of the apartment. I had to stare at the Chinese silk wall coverings, familiarising myself with each flower motif. From the next room, I could hear the tussle of fabrics, the forced expirations at the tightening of corset laces, and a waft of perfume making its way towards me, mixing with the mildew smell from the autumn humidity on the walls. Fortunately, I spotted a text on a small gueridon across the room, and I took the liberty of picking it up to occupy the time."

"Ah—one of Chloë's other lovers is an author?"

"She would not have had the indiscretion to leave it out! It was her handwriting."

George raised an eyebrow and grinned. "Ah! So your belle is an author then!"

"Indeed she is." Nicolas smiled. "The text related the story of how she had landed in the Palais-Royal, an autobiographical account, not altogether without literary merit. She writes how her mother, Anne Fouquet, had provided Chloë with the apartment on the bel étage of the newly developed annex of the Palais-Royal, close to where her own mother Claire had first sung for the regent—and fallen asleep on the duke's lap. The text is not quite balanced, with iffy spelling, but a compelling tale nevertheless. The fame of Mademoiselle Anne Fouquet's attractions had put her in the sights of de Pompadour. Anne's great beauty and sharp tongue led her to be recruited for the Parc-aux-Cerfs carousel, which the Marquise de Pompadour organised for her royal lover."

"That is a lot of behind-the-scenes organisation. Is that how it really works? I suppose she would know with such a family history," interrupted George.

Nicolas acknowledged that it was quite an industry and continued: "Unusually, Louis XV had spent an entire week with Anne, returning each evening. With her six nights of fame behind her, Anne shared the fate of her own mother and received a substantial reward of five hundred thousand pounds the following month. This left her well short of the league of the great courtisanes of the century who amassed enormous wealth, but it did provide the family a measure of social buoyancy."

One of the servants stopped by their table to refresh the damask, fill their cups of champagne, and replenish the plate of deep-purple thinly sliced sausages. Merely a boy, his coarse accent contrasted with a strikingly elegant face, albeit with teeth blackened from neglect and poor diet. The Café de Foy always strove to help children from the countryside escape ruin in the underbelly of Paris, but at the same time Mathilde was a hard taskmaster in the firm conviction that discipline was the gateway to societal success. Those who met her standard often went on to make a life for themselves, sometimes with a small café on the outskirts that she might help finance.

When the boy had moved on to the table beside theirs, Nicolas pursued his history lesson. "Louis XV's first great and sustained affection had been for Madame de Pompadour, Jeanne-Antoinette de Poisson, who was of modest origins. Her father had been a squire to the regent, the Duc d'Orléans. Boucher captured the swirling tones of her beauty. Her insatiable intellectual interests captivated the king, who had elevated her to become the Marquise de Pompadour. One of her many contributions to the Versailles court—and a sorely needed improvement—was an elevated sense of hygiene, with bidets, regular baths, and even a silver toothbrush. Tactful, she was always careful not to unduly embarrass the queen, even after being anointed the official mistress of the king."

"A toothbrush?"

"Indeed." Nicolas smiled. "Like a small shoe brush, to which you apply a paste of ground eggshell, or in the case of the marquise, ground lobster shell, and with a bit of water you rub it back and forth over your teeth."

"But why?"

"Some say that one's teeth remain healthier, but for most the appeal is to have a more pleasant smell on your breath when other lips are in proximity. I will bring you such a brush and powder when we next meet."

George laughed. "I look forward to brushing teeth!"

Nicolas continued: "In any case, the Marquise de Pompadour was to have a lasting influence on the Enlightenment, using part of the immense fortune bestowed on her by Louis XV to support some of the leading thinkers of the time. Voltaire, Charles Pinot Duclos, Montesquieu, Helvétius, Bernard de Fontenelle all passed through her salons and enjoyed her generosity. Her salon at the Hôtel d'Evreux in Paris, another gift from the king, became a veritable catalyst for fresh thinking.[31] Not content to be merely an observer of history, she founded a long line of salons where women participated in debates and midwifed the ideas of the century. Although a formidable woman, several difficult childbirths had made it impossible for her to continue to satisfy the considerable royal libido from 1750, at a mere twenty-nine years of age.[32]

"Avoiding exile to a convent as had been the custom for royal mistresses and continuing to capture at least the ear and

31 Now known as Palais de l'Élysée, the residence and office of the French presidency.

32 Ironically, by encouraging rational thought to displace revealed truth, she had a hand in the ultimate downfall of the house of Bourbon. This was to lead to the decapitation of Louis XVI, the grandson and successor of her own royal lover.

spirit of the king, she continued to live at Versailles—alternating with lengthy stays at the chateaux de Crecy, la Celle, and Menars—all gifts from the king. No longer able to satisfy the king's ardours, in 1755, she set up the house of Parc-aux-Cerfs for him to spend his nights away from the gossiping eyes of the court—as well as to keep his body entirely in her platonic grip. Eventually Louis XV would settle on Madame du Barry as his favourite for the last phase of his life. Dozens of women and girls paraded through the boudoirs of the Parc-aux-Cerfs, from the highest nobility to the lowest provincial ranks of society, all under the tight supervision of the Marquise de Pompadour."

George summarised, "A family tradition, how delightful, but what is the story of the grandmother on the Orléans lap?"

"The manuscript describes this on another set of pages. Chloë d'Avigny was said to have taken after her grandmother Claire, who had made a brief and inconclusive appearance in 1716 at one of the libertine evenings that Philippe Duc d'Orléans held with remarkable constancy in the family palace itself, located at the head of the new Palais-Royal complex.[33] Chloë goes on to describe how King Louis XV was only six years old at the time, and his uncle Philippe had held the regency since the death of Louis XIV, the Roi Soleil, the prior year. The child-king had been installed across the street from the Palais-Royal, in the Louvre. Philippe was married to Mademoiselle de Blois, his cousin, the worldly Princess of Bourbon and one of the

33 Some of this story is extracted from a combination of romanticised and historical details from Vergé-Franceschi, 2015.

eight children of Louis XIV and his mistress Madame de Montespan. Mademoiselle de Blois was to pass on the baton of her own mother as a royal consort by introducing Madame de Pompadour at Versailles in 1745, to be anointed the official mistress of Louis XV. But Philippe had a voracious appetite for debauchery that Mademoiselle de Blois could only temporarily satisfy. The death of Louis XIV in 1715 had lifted the austere discipline of the later Versailles court, particularly after the Sun King had finally settled down with Madame de Maintenon, a deeply religious woman as well as his mistress—and likely secret spouse of forty-two years. After his reign was over, liberated from the king's late-life rediscovery of puritan morals, Paris was now free to go where its untethered instincts would take it. And the Duc d'Orléans would lead the way. D'Orléans was also a gifted musician and had contributed to Gervais's opera *Hypermnestre*."

"We saw *Hypermnestre* only last year," recollected George. "I had not realised an Orléans had helped compose it. It was quite a gruesome libretto. But I do fondly recall the wonderful Te Deum. But how do Chloë's ancestors feature in this opera?"

Nicolas described how, after the opera had just premiered in one of the theatres of the Palais-Royal, Marie-Madeleine de la Vieuville, Comtesse de Parabère, had convened a celebration in honour of the part-time composer and her long-time lover.

"Madame de Parabère had ordered the guests to come in Greek costumes," Nicolas explained, "in keeping with the theme of the opera. The opera's Hypermnestre had been one of the fifty daughters of King Danaos, who wed the fifty sons of King Egyptos. But Danaos had instructed his daughters to kill their husbands on the wedding night, which only Hypermnestre refused to carry out. She saved her husband Lynceus who had honoured her wish to remain a virgin. As a surprise for the easily bored Orléans, Madame de Parabère had imagined a surprise for her own Lynceus. Depicting a Greek statue, Claire had mesmerised the salon as she strode in unselfconsciously, a dagger in her hand as her only costume, singing the aria from the second scene of the fourth act: *'Ma vertu gémissante / Ne peut plus soutenir ces perfides concerts.'*[34]

"Reportedly Claire had been a striking appearance, with a long red braid, adolescent breasts, and distant green eyes, offset by a pale complexion superficially scarred by a bout of small-pox that she had been fortunate to shake off early and which the candlelight mercifully hid. But it was her singular bearing that struck the assembly, grounded in a confidence built from a year on the stage and harvesting the sustained admiration of the Paris elites. Making her way across the room, as instructed by Madame de Parabère, Claire landed on Orléans's lap at the closing line '*C'est lui mon époux.*'[35]

"Champagne flowed richly, and while most of the guests had joined Claire in her Hellenic state of undress, the young

---

34 My groaning virtue / Bears no longer these treacherous sounds. Source: Gervais, 1716.

35 It is he, my husband.

girl herself had fallen asleep, not accustomed to the copious quantities of alcohol. Madame de Parabère had intended her as a surprise for Orléans and as a foil to turn her own attentions elsewhere that evening, albeit under Orléans's salubrious gaze. This time he was content to observe the ardours of amor; witnessing their writhings was its own reward. He let Claire sleep.

"Thus, while Claire had narrowly avoided being compromised in the twilight of the regent's debaucheries, she had also missed out on the fortune that even an occasional courtisane could obtain from submitting to a wealthy aristocrat. Touched by her naïve youthfulness, and flattered by her rendering of his own music, Orléans had nevertheless sent ten thousand pounds the next day and a small set of pearls. This gift at least had the merit of providing an exit from the ever-present danger for actresses of sinking into the lowest ranks of society, and enabling a wedding to a certain Monsieur Fouquet, a notary whose narrow interests provided Claire an opportunity to broaden her own. As we've seen, Claire's own daughter and Chloë's mother, Mademoiselle Anne Fouquet, was to wander closer to the fire, but like her mother, escaped from being consumed completely."

"Quite a pedigree in the profession across several generations. But how attached are you to this girl? She certainly kept you waiting, if you had time to read through this entire tale." George suspected that Nicolas's sharp mind overshadowed a romantic inclination that made him vulnerable to a deeper involvement, a mechanism not unfamiliar to himself.

"She took her time. I've wondered about a more permanent attachment," murmured Nicolas.

"Surely a marquis cannot wed a Chloë."

"Of course. I was more wondering whether you might prepare her in your atelier."

"Really, marquis, that's not at all funny."

"But it is a serious question."

"It is most definitely not a serious question! It is a juvenile fantasy, soaked in copious champagne, which you apparently imbibed in good measure before uttering this absurd idea."

"Of course it is, but indulge me for a moment. Can we at the very least pursue this as a thought experiment? To do so, we must put aside the ethics of cutting short a human life, which is anyway an argument that is trotted out at opportune moments, and equally conveniently suppressed when it gets in the way. We poison our friends with alacrity when they commit some imagined sin, we slaughter the peasants of neighbouring countries with impunity and then proceed to celebrate their butchers as heroes of the Nation, and, who knows, the so-called revolutionaries preaching a new free and just society will no doubt have few compunctions in sending all of us to the guillotine simply to realise their new Jerusalem. So yes, it is juvenile, but less than what we commonly practice, and more than what we otherwise preach. So, is it possible?"

George smiled and felt himself seduced once more by the familiar unorthodoxy of Nicolas's mind, an unorthodoxy that often unshackled him from the dead weight of daily life. Wandering through forbidden and suppressed alleys of thought inevitably triggered new connections. Enlarging the space of ideas allowed them to recompose themselves in new ways, dancing a quadrille with each other until they crystallised in a fresh pattern. It was nothing but refreshing.

George sighed good naturedly. "Well, for one, I have no intention of stripping off the delicate skin of Chloë, submitting it to a treatment of chemical baths, and stretching it across a core that Jeanne would undoubtedly expertly sculpt—all to eternalise the radiance of the marquis's *rousse* with the lustre of a fox fur."

"But can it be done?" insisted Nicolas.

"Very well. Yes, practically speaking, it can, but we should explore the teleology of this idiotic idea. When preparing the queen's zebra, I wished for the viewer to glimpse the wildness that contrasts it with the horse. I want him to shudder at the power of natural forces that are beyond man's control, and I also want him to be seduced by the beauty of the zebra's shape, its shine, and its bearing. What is your Chloë sosie for, exactly?"

"Thank you," muttered Nicolas, settling back in his chair and looking quite relieved now that George was playing along.

Getting used to the idea, George pursued it further. "I'm not so sure. We have such a deep sense of the human form, with much greater sensitivity than for animals: the waiver of a lip, the shimmer in an eye, the fluttering of an eyebrow, the flaring of a nostril. The fleeting dynamics that translate into our own emotions, all that would be gone."

Nicolas leaned forward, his face intentionally more expressive than usual as he asked his next question. "Are you implying human beauty is more defined by its dynamics than animal beauty?"

"Perhaps not, but our standards are much higher or merely our senses better trained on humans, most particularly in your case. You are not after a shape or a symbol but looking to fill a missing piece inside of your soul. Damn your mother for keeping you in juvenile robes for a decade."

"Leave my mother out of it."

"Her hardness would've been easier to capture."

"Yes—and then I can put my stuffed mother in a niche on the stairs."

"That would have raised some awkward questions. Where will you put Chloë when I would be done?"

"Probably in a faraway attic. The constant sight of her would distract me from my work and darken my mood."

"A rather low return on an enterprise, as some social philosopher might have observed."

"Touché."

"Sculpture, or painting, might be more felicitous paths. Or have her ennobled and wed her. And anyway, what has gotten into you with this fantasy? Usually, you are the gentlest of men, a theoretician of the flesh, pronouncing your conviction of the absolute equality of genders even in the presence of ears that had better be deaf."

"Yes, yes. It is just an experiment in my mind—in our minds now. Where is the limit between nature and man? How does our reasoning shift when we consider one realm or the other? Our American friend Jefferson keeps vacillating in our discussions on the rights of men. He evades when I quote the principles of their own constitution of seventy-six, and when I insist that they extend to negroes, his logical mind agrees, but then the politician and perhaps the landed gentleman rebuts. Jefferson has even taken to heart my musings on slavery, which I wrote under the pseudonym of Joachim Schwartz.[36] I'm considering publishing it again, having sharpened my arguments against his agreeable evasions."

"How did we get from red to Schwartz?"

"We are part of nature and yet separate from it." Nicolas continued unperturbed. "But we choose where to set the boundary. The boar can be slaughtered for dinner, the Black man worked to death, and the redhead stuffed?"

"Are you saying that therefore we can do either all or none of these things?"

"Yes—or we are separate from nature. You cannot take both positions. And the tragedy of those who conserve animals is that they attempt to approach nature by controlling her," pursued Nicolas. "Perhaps we should limit ourselves to transforming the living, instead of attempting to bridge to the realm of the dead?"

Sensing that the restless mind of his friend had moved onto another subject but encouraged that his raised chin betrayed a more cheerful impulse than his morbid infatuation with Chloë, George raised a curious eye.

---

36 Jefferson would translate into English Condorcet's 'Réflections sur l'esclavage des nègres,' written under the pseudonym Schwartz in 1781.

Nicolas changed the subject. "I was rather charmed by your Jeanne's metamorphosis into a man. A striking appearance, which several members had noted. The boundaries between social classes can be as rigid as those with the afterworld, but she appears able to scale them with ease. I'd be curious to try that once more."

"Take her out with us to the Palais-Royal? I'm not sure she would appreciate that, and her attractions would be difficult to protect. Boundaries are entertaining to probe, but just as I was reticent to disembowel Chloë's body, I feel an urge to protect both Jeanne's spirits and her modesty."

Nicolas reassured him that his intentions were more playful than sinister and asked whether he thought Jeanne might accompany him sometime to a ball, where she could be introduced, perhaps as an obscure princess from the house of Savoie. "Let's see if a little bit of instruction, combined with her keen sense of observation, make the social boundaries evaporate."

Amused by the idea of Jeanne blurring the social order as a princess, George suggested that they enlist Mathilde to help order appropriate apparel.

"Splendid!" exclaimed Nicolas, relieved that his friend had been willing to join him in his labyrinth. "And my sister can provide the necessary training for Jeanne. She takes her position as a marquise with an earnestness bordering on pomposity, but at the same time has a keen sense of humour. She will most certainly see the charm of this subterfuge. Additionally, the hostess of the evening that I envision taking Jeanne to, has had the temerity to enter a great rivalry with my sister, who will therefore most certainly savour the idea of tricking her."

George chuckled at the idea. But while he admired the aristocratic ease with which Nicolas would play with norms and values, he simultaneously worried about Jeanne not becoming a playball to their whims. They should speak about it first.

7

The Robbery

A week after the unveiling of the zebra, a persistent mid-morning autumnal drizzle hung in the air, wrapping the red and ochre trees in a humid haze. Few walkers had left the relative comfort of their houses, and the others were mostly workers speeding to their destinations. The fog slightly muffled the sounds of George's footsteps on the hard ground. He had intended to take a long walk westwards along the bank of the Seine to clear his mind. It was also a long-ago established daily habit he had formed together with Violette, the enduring routine of which seemed to amplify her presence a little. But beset by hesitation after a mere fifteen minutes, he doubled back to the rue des Saints-Pères.

In the courtyard stood an unfamiliar fiacre flanked by two men in long dark blue coats with the double row of brass buttons and triangular hats of the Paris police. Although apparently just waiting, their rod-straight bearing betrayed an intent to project fortitude. They stared at George as he stepped through the large doors. He was startled by their stern stance and crossed arms, and the swords that hung at their sides. The policemen appeared to intently study this apparition in a dark grey cape—for that was how George imagined himself on this dreary morning—who had just entered their field of observation. Deducing, George assumed, from his intentionally unhesitant gait that he was the master of the house, they curtly nodded and motioned him towards the entrance door.

George climbed the stairs two steps at a time, slowing just before entering the room with as much aplomb as he could muster. A tall man in a black coat was standing next to the fireplace, interrogating the portrait of Violette to its right with a concentrated stare. George recognised him as Inspecteur Lenoir. His confident poise thrust his chest forward, causing his chin—covered with a short-trimmed beard—to bear slightly downwards. Weathered and worn tall military boots added a nice touch of imperfection. George wondered whether this inconsistent dress aimed to frighten and reassure his prey at the same time.

Inspecteur Lenoir turned his gaze away from the portrait and fixed his eyes on George. "Are you familiar with the doctrine of chance, Monsieur du Paon?"

"Yes—it is what one turns to at the game tables. But what—"

"And are you familiar with the reverend Bayes?"

“I’m afraid not.”

“A dour man, but an interesting one for our purposes today.”

“And may I enquire as to the purpose of your visit?”

Ignoring George, the policeman continued: “In 1763, two years after his death, the Royal Society of London published a remarkable essay under the title ‘An Essay towards Solving a Problem in the Doctrine of Chances.’ In it, he treats a question that is at the heart of every police enquiry. When you see a boy throwing a paving stone at a window, it is easy to conclude that the glass was broken through the force of the stone, and therefore one can readily deduce that the guilty party is the boy. But the police are mostly faced with the opposite problem. One finds a broken window and the police are asked to deduce the cause. You will concede that this is the much more challenging problem. We policemen cannot afford the luxury of scientists who believe that every problem has an exact solution and that the only issue is finding enough data for logic to lead us to it. In our work, that is never the case, as the information is always incomplete—not only in practice but also in principle. So we accept that we must reason using incomplete information, and that is where the reverend Bayes’s writings have proven an invaluable source of guidance.”

“So how exactly is the Scottish reverend helpful for your work? The problem itself sounds familiar, as I have often wondered whether our friend Descartes’s idea of the world as a clock is accurate enough, but in the absence of assuming a divine justification for every detail, it seems that we don’t have much choice.” George drew upon his most recent scientific dilemma in the hope that Lenoir might be more forthcoming as to the nature of his visit. "What is in a zebra that is not in a donkey," George asked, "and are there any specific facts that can make clear the cause of their differences?"

The policeman avoided the bait and proceeded to expand somewhat pedantically on his explorations of Bayes.

"You see," the inspecteur pursued, "Bayes is always on my mind. Recently, I had a robbery case, a stolen bracelet, I recall. The object is not important. One of our habitual police informers led us to the house of the purported criminal. We searched his rooms and found the stolen object. I might have closed the case, but it all seemed too simple, the correlation between the crime and the purported criminal seemed too direct. Police intuition one might call it, and I wondered what Bayes might have thought. My men brought the suspect's family to the police station, and we grilled our informer. Gradually, we discovered that our suspect was being blackmailed, whereupon he had threatened to warn us. To avoid that, our informer had planted the evidence, counting on his usefulness to us to keep him above suspicion. We solved the case to my satisfaction thanks to Bayesian logic. It appears that context matters more than linear causality."

"So have you posted two men in front of my house to have a conversation about uncertainty and logic? I much appreciate the trouble and the honour, but I'm afraid others would be better sparring partners for you." George could not help taking a liking to the freedom of the policeman's unconstrained, although disciplined, mind.

Lenoir paced around the room, positioning himself in front of the window so that the sunlight reduced him to his contour.

"Forgive me, Monsieur du Paon. I have even omitted to introduce myself. Lenoir is my name, which I believe may be familiar to you?"

"Indeed, Inspecteur Lenoir," George replied. "My good friend the Marquis de Condorcet has reason to be grateful to you for saving him from embarrassment or worse at a time when his otherwise considerable judgement failed him utterly. You saved Condorcet from embarrassment over the abduction of the eighteen-year-old Mademoiselle de Boubers he was infatuated with, the niece of my friend Madame Amélie Suard. A sordid affair, which you handled admirably, although I dread to think what would have happened if Nicolas had not had the ancestry that he has."

"The Greeks represented justice as blind, but that would make it difficult to solve any case with adequate consideration of social stability."

George marvelled at the veil of irony that seemed to radiate from the policeman's face. His eyebrows raised in a frozen frown had drawn deep-carved, undulating furrows on his tall forehead. This in turn shifted his thick black hair farther upwards. Lenoir's authority made him appear taller than he was. His hands were particularly expressive. A tight pinching of thumb and index together on his right hand, raising his other fingers, reminded George of a mudra he had studied in drawings of the Buddha, when he had been working on a large monkey whose hands had defied expression. Lenoir's solemn gesture was his way of extracting attention from his audience.

The taxidermist pursued, "Perhaps that is why Cesare Beccaria argued to separate police from justice?"

"Touché, Monsieur du Paon, but perhaps we should turn to your problem."

"And how exactly would you describe my problem?"

"A certain property of the Queen of England appears to have disappeared from your premises, and as you just alluded to, although the species is reputed to be untameable, it is unlikely to have galloped along the Seine with the quantity of chemicals you have soaked her in," Lenoir announced, and George had the distinct impression that the inspecteur was almost salivating at the effect his words had on his host.

Agitated by this sudden news and sensing that his carefully shaped world was melting ever so slightly, George slowly sat down in the large leather chair by the fireplace. With a sudden surge of emptiness in his chest, he took several long breaths before speaking. "Forgive me, but I find that hard to believe. My staff is always present in the house. How have you come to know about this—and where are Jeanne and Gaston anyway?"

His brow frowning farther, the inspecteur gave a quick nod and, ignoring the first question, answered, "My men are having a conversation with each of them—separately, naturally—at the Châtelet police headquarters."

At the thought of Jeanne being interrogated by police—and Gaston, too—George felt his stomach do a flip. "Can you assure me that they are being treated well?" he enquired. "I trust them completely and cannot fathom that they would be involved in any nefarious scheme. You will forgive me for worrying, but there have been occasions when the police are reputed to not be universally gentle with witnesses."

Lenoir smiled knowingly. "I can assure you that you need not worry about your staff, since I agree that it is most unlikely that they are the authors of the disappearance, but I must still confirm whether they heard or saw anything—and formally exclude any collaboration with less well-intended people."

"But how did you know the zebra had been stolen?" George repeated his first question. "What led you here? Who alerted you?"

"It is our business to know. In matters that concern the court and its relationship with other courts, and it is our business to know before anyone else knows."

"While your response further confirms the high regard with which I already hold the police, it is not particularly informative," George grumbled. The policeman's self-satisfaction was adding to his growing irritation—he realised the ramifications for himself if he could not return the zebra to London, and surely the officer must have considered them as well. He had always viewed political intrigue as something to observe and discuss but now dreaded becoming its fodder. A heightened fear further sharpened his analytical reflexes. "Tell me, Monsieur Lenoir, if you knew about this before myself or anyone in my household, why did you not have it stopped?"

The inspecteur smiled contentedly, savouring the effect of his words as if he were swallowing a fine oyster. "It is correct,

Monsieur du Paon, that your commission for England was known to us, and due to the complicated relationship between our countries, we thought it best to survey your house around the clock. After your presentation at the Académie and the interest it raised, we doubled the surveillance."

"I had no idea," George murmured.

"Yes, well, my men report that a chariot entered your house this morning for what appeared like a normal delivery of wood. About twenty minutes later, the horses reappeared, pulling out the chariot, now relieved of its load. One of the policemen with a sharper eye noticed that the horses were particularly finely groomed and bridled, in a way that was incongruous with wood delivery. He also observed that there was something large in the chariot where the wood had been, a rather sizeable object bundled in heavy blankets. Before the policeman could share this with his colleague, the convoy bolted at high speed down the street, spurred by the outstanding horses and the light load. The men pursued the chariot on foot, but quickly lost its track as it sped westward along the Seine."

George slumped a little deeper in his chair, considering the implications. Setting aside his failure to have noticed that the police continuously watched his house, the burning wood in the chimney took on a different glow, as if it had become a passive accomplice to the theft. The refined origin of the horses indicated that the zebra was likely not being held for ransom. This was a relief, as he would not be dragged into a vulgar criminal enterprise, although paying to recover his work seemed the simpler resolution. On the other hand, if it were indeed a political plot, it would be much harder to untangle. He thought back to the diamonds of Madame du Barry and how this murky affair had stained the reputation of many at court—and indeed continued to diminish Queen Marie Antoinette in the eyes of the public. Emerging from his ruminations, George asked Lenoir whether there was already a suspect.

"By necessity, there is always a suspect, as we need one to resolve the case. The question is rather whether he is a guilty suspect or merely a convenient suspect."

"I guess I would be a convenient non-guilty suspect."

"You have friends in high places—in part because of that you are not a very attractive suspect, even discounting the fact that people would wonder why you stole your own zebra."

"Can I suggest we apply the methods of your friend Mr. Bayes to find the most guilty instead of the most convenient suspect? Much more gratifying also." George fixed a steady gaze on Lenoir. "You are a resourceful man—whom do you suspect?"

Lenoir gave George an intense and thoughtful stare before replying, "You, Monsieur du Paon, have created an extraordinary object, which appears to have the effect of disclosing the origin of the zebra's wildness, at least to sensitive observers of its form. Access to knowledge through observation and not through deduction is troubling to the authorities, and, given the English penchant for empiricism, it is an aspect some are loath to strengthen."

Lenoir clearly knew a great amount of detail on the discussions after the presentation of the zebra at the Académie, notwithstanding the strictly closed nature of the meeting.

Either he had heard the deliberations from a hidden location, or more likely from one of the *Académiciens*, having been obligated by some undisclosed scandal to report extensively to the police. In any case, Lenoir did not share his suspicions with George.

Excusing himself, Lenoir turned and left the room. George discerned some muted instructions to the men in the courtyard; the gate to the street opened with lighter incoming footsteps and boots marching out. To his relief, a whistling tune and an asymmetric click could be heard in the courtyard, and he recalled that he had seen Jeanne repair one of her heels with a metal clip from the workshop.

8

The Americans in Paris

The Marquis de Condorcet's carriage entered the courtyard of the hotel at 59 rue d'Auteuil in Passy, the freshly minted Princess de Savoie at his side in an olive shot silk dress with a riot of embroidered delicate roses, pansies, and carnations tied with a bow. From his vantage point on the first floor, his cheekbone pressed against the glass pane, George could discern the glitter of the narrow emerald necklace from the Condorcet family, which distracted from a plunging contemporary décolleté. He glimpsed the wide red-gold band around the princess's wrist, constituted of thousands of diminutive golden feathers, each hooked in an underlying mesh of golden wire. The bracelet undulated like a golden fleece with every flip of the wrist. It had been a present for Violette a few years earlier, and it felt bittersweet to see it worn again.

Jeanne had been reticent about Nicolas's idea when George had first proposed it to her, but she was quickly won over by the potential for wider social exploration following her experience at the Académie. Mathilde Joussereau's tailor had designed a fitting garment, buoyed by Nicolas's means and enthusiasm. Despite his distraction over the zebra, George had found the visits of Nicolas's sister to the atelier both amusing and entertaining—she spent several afternoons teaching Jeanne to walk with a heavy book on her head and introducing her to the quirks and habits of her class, while ensuring that a whiff of provincialism would prevail. They extensively practiced the facial expression at rest, which Nicolas's sister insisted must at all times convey the sense of contentedness and confidence in what may lie ahead, an expression that uniquely characterises the aristocracy. An afternoon performance in George's appartement under the watchful gaze of Nicolas had convinced them that Jeanne was ready for the stage.

George imagined that, as they progressed to the east of Paris, Jeanne would fidget with the small bag that held the rouge and powder for the evening, a foreign presence in her hands. Her fingers might trace the hard core of the cardboard structure covered with silk, following the sinuous lines of the curved bottom, exploring the hollow side panels separated by sharp straight edges and settling on its padded top. A nervous shake of the head might test the physics of the constraining structures of the elaborate hair pyramid, the movement releasing whiffs of perfume and powder within the narrow enclosure of the carriage. Nicolas would attempt to distract and reassure Jeanne with anecdotes of previous gatherings at the rue d'Auteuil, which would serve to increase her wonderment at the world she was about to enter. Perhaps having chosen the wrong approach, he might switch to expressing admiration at her talents, as an artist in chasing a representation of the wildness of nature, as a social observer at the Académie, and at her good-natured jousts with Mathilde during the fitting sessions with Mathilde's tailor and his own sister. From his vantage point in the rue d'Auteuil, George imagined Nicolas and Jeanne's journey and how the bag might finally come to rest on stacked silk folds atop Jeanne's knees. Her feet would continue to complain bitterly, not being accustomed to being squeezed into overly narrow lasts, but during the fittings, George had convinced her that such was the fate of a princess.

The awning above the entrance to the carriageway shielded them from the autumn drizzle. Being stuck in his distant perch, not without a pinch of envy, George saw the marquis and the princess walk up the stairs past the uniformed footmen who held open the doors. It was a familiar destination for Nicolas, though George imagined that this familiarity was of small comfort—Nicolas now needed to make a plausible introduction of an unfamiliar face, trusting that her avidness to soak up the new would seduce the audience.

Madame Helvétius's salon La Société d'Auteuil was not only an occasion to discuss progressive ideas and contest social conventions in pleasant surroundings, but also to follow the developments of American revolutionary society and politics, as their envoys were amongst the regular guests.

Along with other salons governed by the pantheon of Parisian women such as Madame Helvétius, Julie de Lespinasse, or the recently wed and youthful Germaine de Staël, the Société d'Auteuil was an integral part of the institutional fabric of the Enlightenment, as they turned from primarily literary to political subjects, midwifing and encouraging increasingly liberal or revolutionary ideas.

The house in the Parisian suburb of Passy belonged to Anne-Catherine de Ligniville d'Autricourt, known as Madame Helvétius or, for fewer, Minette. In the fifteen years since her husband, the philosopher Claude-Adrien Helvétius, had passed away, she had combined the large fortune he had harnessed through his lucrative efforts as a tax collector with her immense capacity to bewitch the male intellect or, more precisely, male intellectuals. Her attraction was less rooted in classic beauty than in the biting wit, liberally waving petticoats, and joyous charisma that led her to consume a steady stream of lovers. At the age of sixty-four, she retained the capacity to charm a room, as George had observed when he had been introduced to her as the replacement of her majordomo Émile who had called in sick that morning.

"It is such a relief that you are able to step in at the last moment, and I am so grateful that Émile was able to suggest and recommend such an experienced replacement."

"It is my pleasure to help, Madame Helvétius. The carnet suggests that you are expecting illustrious guests," responded George, standing rod straight as he had often observed his new brethren do.

"I am very grateful. My staff is experienced and competent, and I should think you will not have much to take care of, but it is so essential to have a more experienced person present to resolve any sudden unexpected events. Naturally you will be adequately rewarded for your efforts today. I understand that Émile will probably be back with us in a few days, at the latest?" Not waiting for a reply, with a curt but heartfelt nod, Madame Helvétius turned and strode through the high gilded double doors into the darkness of the next room.

In preparation for his impromptu new role as a head servant, George had spent a day in the reading room in the Palais-Royal to acquaint himself as much as possible with his temporary employer. In one of the periodicals, he had noted that the rather prudish Mrs. Adams, newlywed to the American ambassador to the court of Saint James, considered Madame Helvétius to be the archetype of the bad French woman—coquette and libertine—as she sat on the lap of her famous neighbour, Benjamin Franklin. Abigail Adams was quoted as having written that as the *seductress-salonnière* "showed more than her foot," she had been "highly disgusted, and never wished for an acquaintance with any ladies of this caste." The journalist described how she was further scandalised when one of the many furry dogs adorned with silk ribbons peed on the floor and Minette mopped it up with her petticoat, while not missing a beat in a complaint about Descartes's overly rigorous approach to logic and how the Scot Bayes had suggested a better path. The periodical characterised Madame Helvétius as utterly unconcerned with conventional social norms but gifted with an insatiable mind, her vitality suggesting that she had discovered access to the fountain of youth. It made her irresistible, at least to those not faint of heart.

After leafing through a stack of superficial society anecdotes, George had stumbled on a journal that described the dalliances of the previous American ambassador to Paris, who had gone home the prior year. Somewhat provocatively using her more informal appellation, the journalist described how Minette appeared to grow younger with age. Franklin had been so taken with her that he had unsuccessfully and repeatedly asked for her hand in marriage, even with a plea set by the amateur printer on his own press titled "To our Lady of Auteuil: A Descent into Hell."[37] Reportedly, she had loved him enough to always pronounce his name with the emphasis on the first syllable, which was no small tribute from a French woman. It was oddly dissonant with her charismatic extroversions and betrayed greater artifice than she otherwise let on. When she once teased him about not spending the night with her, Franklin had countered: "Madame, I am waiting until the nights are longer." Madame Helvétius and Franklin mirrored each other's boundless curiosity, as well as both being ardently sought after amorously by many. They delighted in each other's company, and marriage was the only thing she withheld from him.

George looked up from the journal, smiling at the playfulness of the age, and at the same time noting his own Violette void. He missed their lighthearted banter, the borderline flirting, their companionship.

---

37 Prioleau, 2003.

The journalist had been thorough, summarising the well-documented life of the famous ambassador. Franklin's wife, who had remained in Boston, had been unschooled and overly practical, reflecting the social class he had since soared from and left her stranded in. But with Minette, he had found an inclination of equals. "Things are badly arranged in this world when I see that two beings, so made to be happy together are obliged to separate," he lamented when leaving for America a year before, following a nine-year stay in Paris. The journal concluded that Franklin was fully aware that Minette's ferocious autonomy was at the heart of her attractiveness and modernity, which a marriage may have paradoxically dulled.

George acutely remembered the confusing state of American diplomacy in Paris over the past decade. As the American ambassador, or rather as one of five American ambassadors, Benjamin Franklin had resided in the Passy property of a rich merchant, Jacques Donatien Le Ray, Comte de Chaumont, with a seven-hectare garden overlooking the Seine. At least four others had been vying for the role of American envoy: Deane and Lee, who had originally travelled with him to Paris in 1776, as well as Lee's brother and Izard, who were intended as ambassadors to Florence and Berlin but ended up marooned in Paris, as those courts were less than enthusiastic about receiving representatives from a government that had seceded through a revolution from a kingdom.

Franklin's international reputation as a scientist and statesman outshone them all, but most importantly, he embodied the spirit of the Enlightenment that held France in thrall. The old man represented the future. Having been single-handedly responsible for securing the financing of the American independence wars through his close relationship with the Comte de Vergennes, Louis XVI's minister of foreign affairs, he felt it was time to return home—leaving his successor Jefferson with the unenviable task of dealing with the gargantuan American debt, as well as backfilling his Olympian reputation. George had heard repeated anecdotes about how Jefferson was flummoxed from seeing every French salon prominently displaying a small bust of his predecessor on their mantlepieces. Franklin was inevitably a hard act to follow for virtually anyone.

Being as prepared as he could be, George now stood in the service corridor connecting the main reception room with the kitchens and service quarters. A small opening provided an unobstructed view, allowing him to assess the performance of the staff and intervene when necessary, as the lackeys and valets entered and exited. From his position, George could see Condorcet and the freshly minted princess entering the large blue-and-white parlour and greeting the Duc de La Rochefoucauld. Nicolas had seen him a week earlier at the Masonic lodge of the Nine Sisters, where Franklin had also been a member. La Rochefoucauld always needed to balance between the intellectual attraction of Minette's assembly and the inconvenience of his allergic reaction to the clowder of sixteen angora cats dressed in coloured satin jackets that wove themselves between the silk-covered legs of the men, assiduously dodging their canine brethren. As George had seen in the carnet, in addition to Franklin's successor, Jefferson, tonight's invitees, carefully composed by Madame Helvétius, included the liberal aristocracy La Fayette and Noailles, along with the writers Chamfort and Saint-Lambert. George admired the thoroughness of the operation of the Helvétius salon, as the carnet contained a short biography of each guest so that the majordomo would be aware of each of their contexts.

Filippo Mazzei, who had been Jefferson's neighbour in Virginia and recently surfaced in France, was in attendance, driven by his constant quest to collect funds for his many plans. The sharply dressed Abbé Morellet, a friend of Franklin and a liberal ecclesiast, who had recently translated the Virginia Act for Establishing Religious Freedom, prized his comfort more than he did his faith, and invested heavily in a lavish wardrobe, mainly in a quest to charm the members of his own gender. Constantin-Francois Chasseboeuf had travelled extensively in Egypt and Syria and was writing a book about his observations on the exoticism of the Levant.[38] Exceptionally, joining a salon other than her own in the rue Bergère, Suzanne Necker had been invited and reminded Condorcet of her daughter Germaine de Staël's commanding presence at the dinner of Couteulx de la Noraye.

George saw that Nicolas now introduced his companion to Mazzei and Chasseboeuf. Mazzei leaned forward as if to absorb her perfume while his nose was on its downward trajectory towards her hand, stopping his lips just short of the surface, perhaps briefly wondering at the coarse surface of her

---

38 Adams, 2000, pp. 144–154.

fingers. Dollops of cream had not been able to transform worker's hands into those of a *salonnière*. But Mazzei, having grown accustomed to the practical habits of women in America, probably did not give it a second thought.

George was delighted that he could not only observe the room, but that the shape of the ceiling vault cascaded the sounds down along the walls, delivering them into his observation window. Thus, he overheard Chasseboeuf singing the praise of the valleys of Savoie, which he had had the occasion to explore scientifically. "Princess, I have the privilege to study the growth of the indigenous flowers in your beautiful mountains!" he exclaimed, prompting Jeanne to change the subject to avoid being queried on the details of her hypothetical home.

"Tell us about America," Jeanne asked Mazzei with the trace of a Savoie accent that she had practiced, visibly startling Nicolas with the ease with which she claimed control of the conversation.

"While the Appalachian Mountains do not rival the Savoie in altitude, dear Princess," Mazzei explained, "their sinuous landscapes capture the imagination. In the autumn, they are transformed into a fiery landscape of orange, mustard, red, and cognac colours as far as the eye reaches. The trees appear to defy winter with an overwhelming last firework of life. As generous as nature is, the inhabitants of the Americas have a tendency towards a dour puritanism, which can drive an Italian to desperation.

"And the food! The food is awful. Mostly enormous quantities of tasteless produce. The death of me. That said, there is no shortage of exceptional specimens who flout the rule. I recall a remarkably premature young boy, John Chapman was his name, whom I met in Massachusetts. In the Western regions of the Americas, he is better known under the name Johnny Appleseed. A virtual orphan, as his mother had died during the childbirth of his brother and his father was away with his regiment, he was obsessed with apple trees. Barely ten years old, he dreamt of travelling west and planting apple trees all over the Americas. It may just have been a childhood fantasy, but sometimes the depth of a child's passion betrays a broader power at work, and one cannot help wondering whether it would not come to pass.[39] The American continent does inspire one to imagine that all ambitions could in principle be realised."

"What about the role of women?" asked Jeanne. As the valets sped past him, George noticed her shoulders lowered themselves imperceptibly, slightly buoying her chest into the grasp of its shot silk barrier. He was increasingly content with his social experiment—he relished seeing Jeanne, so gently determined to mine her fleeting princessdom for all it was worth.

Momentarily raising an eyebrow, Mazzei continued. "More than in France, women bow to a rigid social order dictated by Christian values. Most certainly outside the main cities, where some exercise considerable freedom not dissimilar to what we know in Paris. A notable difference is that this freedom is not

39 John Chapman (1774–1845) became known as Johnny Appleseed and is credited for single-handedly rooting the apple into American folklore, spreading them into every frontier homestead, bringing a rare taste of sweetness into their lives through cider and apple pie—although a bit later than our story.

dictated by the privilege of birth, but apparently by the power of their personality and talents. I have known remarkable painters, hotel keepers, and even manufacturers. But I fear this thought may unsettle a princess such as yourself?"

"Quite the contrary, Monsieur Mazzei, my privileged upbringing has not kept me from realising that worth and birth are not necessarily correlated. It is quite intriguing to have an open mind. Perhaps even a lowly worker could one day exceed the worth of a princess? That would be amusing."

Mazzei smiled and gave Condorcet a puzzled look before taking his leave from the princess and walking over to a small group gathered around the American ambassador.

The contrast between Jefferson's appearance and his predecessor could not have been starker. Franklin cultivated the image of the sober American Quaker, consistently dressed in a loosely fitting long brown coat and a beaver hat in the winter—no silks, ribbons, or heels. Seated next to him, the Marquise de Créquy had described her disdain for the printer and bookseller: "He had long hair like a seminarian from Quimper; he wore a brown suit, a brown vest, and brown breeches of the same cloth, and his hands were of the same colour; he wore a red-striped cravat."[40]

This was, George could only assume, not only to emphasise the great need for money that his country petitioned for at the French court, but also a deliberate strategy of allowing the established elites to feel a step above him. As a parvenu,

---

40 Créquy, 1839, p. 179.

George understood that he must have always been acutely aware of the importance of not outshining the nobility, whose acceptance implicitly relied on their comfort in his acquiescence of their more rightful place. Entirely tactical and accompanied by a clear-headed understanding of his superiority in most other respects, this had served him well. He understood how to dominate from below. Ever since he had decided to transition from worker to gentleman in 1748 by selling his business, this had been his rule. To punctuate the transition, the first portrait he had commissioned from Robert Feke expressed this clearly. It depicts a somewhat stiff figure in a black coat with a most neutral expression, his right hand open and pointing to the ground, the left hand tucked in his coat, the background two-thirds understated black and one-third a mountain landscape. While Franklin was a sober but exuberant global celebrity, Jefferson was more of an observer of society rather than its central actor. They shared a keen interest in the Enlightenment, as readers and debaters, as well as through their own extensive writings.

Ever since he had joined Franklin in Paris as Minister Plenipotentiary in 1784, the contrast between the two men had been on clear display. Jefferson was entirely comfortable matching Parisian nobility, albeit as the more modest dresser amongst them. The Southern landed family that he issued from had given him the confidence to wear a customary bright red coat, his clothes fitting so tightly as to border on dandiness. The bills from his London tailors amply demonstrated the importance he placed on dressing well, blending in as a Frenchman, although without the extravagant Versailles touches, where courtiers adorned rows of ribbons and medals to flaunt their importance.

It was far from obvious that he might fit in. The circumstances and culture of the landed elites in Virginia did not bear any comparison to the sophistication of Parisian society. Virginia was fundamentally rural, mostly populated by uneducated farmers and more slaves. But his father had taken care to expose his son to the classics and even acquire some French at an early age—a fortuitous investment. His legal studies at William and Mary had exposed him to the full breadth of Scottish and French Enlightenment writing.

As at the Société d'Auteuil this evening, one of the habits he had adopted at the Hôtel de Langeac—his Parisian residence in the rue de Berri originally built for the Marquise de Langeac, the mistress of the Comte de Saint-Florentin—and later continued in Washington and at Monticello, was setting up dinners at small tables, where the guests, unusually, served themselves. George knew that his underlings for the night—often padding their earnings by spying for a rival or the police—would only be called in to bring new courses and clear away, but they were out of earshot when politically or philosophically sensitive discussions would be held. In his preparatory reading for the night, George had learnt how, at other salons, this offered the chance for amorous explorations, one aspect of French society that Jefferson struggled with. The article even quoted Jefferson's correspondence: "Intrigues of love occupy the younger, and those of ambition, the elder part of the great. Conjugal love having no existence among them, domestic happiness of which that is the basis, is utterly unknown."[41] Also this distinguished him from his predecessor, who had no such qualms.

George saw how, standing between the large bay windows, Jefferson commanded the attention of a small group of Minette's guests. "This summer, in the delightful company of John and Abigail Adams, I admired the English hand at gardening," he professed.

With a curved wave of his hand sketching a reverence, Mazzei proceeded: "Madame Adams is a charming creature but trusts more strongly in the guidance of her priest than in the desires of the heart, let alone the flesh. I can imagine English gardens capture her interest, as they simulate nature in a protected setting, both taking away the hand of God, and exiling the heart of man. Vauxhall Pleasure Gardens excepted, although a mere shadow of your Palais-Royal, and to both of which she most certainly objects.[42] As the Vauxhall ballad confirms: 'Women squeak and men drunk fall / Sweet enjoyment of Vauxhall.' Curious, that both the French and British cauldrons of pleasure were created by royals, the Comte d'Orléans and the Prince of Wales. In fact, I have taken a rather strong dislike to Mrs. Adams, who reminds me of everything I abhor in the Calvinist rigours of Virginia."

Jefferson ignored the sneer and pursued his original trajectory. "Woburn Farm, Caversham, Wotton, Stow, Edgehill, Stratford upon Avon, Birmingham, the Leasowes, Hagely, Stourbridge,

---

41 Adams, 2000, p. 21.

42 Meghi, "London's Centre of Intrigue and Scandal."

Worcester, Woodstock, Blenheim, Oxford—all delightfully balanced gardens, proudly framing nature in Arcadian perfection."[43] La Fayette noted the irony that Jefferson should succumb to Anglomania, having fought for independence from it.

The abbé considered that Le Nôtre's firm hand would be a better inspiration for the nation of Enlightenment. "At least he does not pretend to reproduce nature, but simply to sculpt with its elements and its vital force in a masculine fashion."

Minette joined the group in a rustle of silk. "Le Nôtre's designs are showing their age," she interjected. "I visited La Rochefoucauld over the summer, and he is thoroughly converted to the Jardin Anglais. And Rousseau also thoroughly disapproved of our stiff gardens." George saw how the duc nodded gratefully, seemingly confirmed in his taste by the lady whose opinion he had learnt to fear.

"Rousseau might have been English, also in his taste for rather youthful amors," observed Chasseboeuf, "or from the Levant on second thought."

Having learnt early on not to follow French conversation into every side alley, Jefferson ignored him and proceeded. "In America, we have such overabundance of plants that we can surpass the English gardens simply through removal instead of having to plant everything."

Nicolas, with the stern look that George knew well, commented to the ambassador that it was interesting to conceive of a garden as the reduction of nature rather than as a creation

43 Adams, 2000, p. 117.

of man. "But," he added, "when is it still nature? Or even a monument to nature? Having removed many parts, is nature still present? One wonders how far one can pursue this, separating and spacing out every individual plant. The Japanese gardens that we know from drawings are wonderfully harmonious but are sometimes entirely void of any life, reduced to compositions of pebbles and rocks. It may well distantly evoke the harmony of nature, but does this exquisite desert really express the essence of the natural world?"

Heading to the corridor to relieve himself outside, Nicolas mistakenly turned into the servant's hallway, resolutely striding past George, momentarily not recognising him in the half-light. Abruptly turning back, he exclaimed with as much self-control as he could muster, "George, by Jupiter! What on earth are you doing here?"

"I couldn't miss this for the world. An infinite improvement on our evenings at the theatre in the Palais-Royal, don't you think?" George replied, smiling broadly, deeply satisfied at having outwitted and surprised his friend.

"But how? What? How did you land into this corridor?" he stammered.

"It was not simple, but as we were metamorphosising Jeanne, I started to think of a plan to attend the evening. Gaston had once boasted that he sometimes was acquainted with a group of majordomos from the great houses of Paris. Anyway, it took a few monetary conversations to convince this certain Émile who works here to feign acute food poisoning for the evening and warmly recommend a temporary replacement."

Looking amused, but obviously fearful that a conversation between a marquis and one of Minette's servants might attract undue attention, and likely hurried by the growing pressure on his bladder, he quickly murmured, "Splendid, well done, but please don't let Jeanne see you. It might unsettle her to the point of losing her lines." Smiling, he sped out.

Nicolas looked surprised upon his return to find Jeanne deep in conversation with the American ambassador, who appeared to be dutifully under her spell. As Nicolas rejoined them, it seemed that Jefferson had discovered that Jeanne was not aware of Lahontan's travel tales from the new world and was recounting the extensive dialogues between the baron and the Indian chief Adario from a century earlier.

Jefferson lectured the princess, "The Baron de Lahontan had joined the French army and had been posted to Canada as a general. He learnt both the Wendat and Algonkian languages—and became good friends with several local Indian leaders. Adario—whose Indian name was Kandiaronk—was particularly outspoken and described by Jesuits as a brilliant orator and man of deep reflection on social norms and the structure of the state. He was a regular valued guest at the table of the governor and Lahontan had befriended him. The baron's open-hearted description of the indigenous cultures of Canada, along with the explicit rendering of the subtle critique of French religion and societal policies, had led to a prolonged exile in Amsterdam."

"Indeed," the marquis commented, "I recall being struck by his books from 1704. *Dialogues de Monsieur le baron de Lahontan et d'un sauvage dans l'Amérique*, I think. Veuve Boeteman in Amsterdam published them. It greatly influenced my own thinking, and his reflections on our European values have been the subject of many debates, as he was so much read."

Jefferson pursued his lesson. "Adario describes money as the source of the social rot in European culture, as people lose their freedom by obsessing with mine and thine. This leads them to prostrate themselves like snakes before some nobleman, who himself is miserable as he navigates between greed for more and unhappiness in the conflicts around him. The French spend their lives in chains instead of living free. Adario does not disdain Europeans, he just feels sorry for them. Lahontan quotes him as having said, 'What kind of human, what species of creature, must European be, that they have to be forced to do good, and only refrain from evil because of fear of punishment?'"

"But don't the Indians have any property of their own?" wondered the ephemeral princess.

"They do not," the ambassador continued. "The Huron share everything, have no laws, no courts, and their chiefs have very limited authority to tell anyone what to do. Again, Adario professed that 'what you call money is the devil of devils; the tyrant of the French, the source of all evils; the bane of souls and slaughterhouse of the living.' Yet their culture has prospered for centuries. Chief Adario was well travelled. He had visited the court of Louis XIV and was acquainted with European culture, yet could not help but pity the state Europeans had found themselves in. He found reading and writing equally useless, as he thought it leads to misunderstandings and falsehoods. A single scrap of paper can ruin a family, as when a woman's letter to her lover lingers. But arithmetic had a different appeal to him as particularly useful for trade—as long as the trader is an honest man."

"What about the role of women in their society?"

"Ah, Princess, I see you have an interest in the place of your own gender." The ambassador pressed the tips of his fingers together, pausing for an instant. "Very well. Indeed, for these savages, men and women have quite different roles than those we are accustomed to. Women choose their husbands, whose attractions are easier to judge, as they go naked instead of being covered by ribbons and silk. They do not need the permission of their parents to choose a spouse; it is their choice. If they are expectant against their desires, the pregnancy is aborted with an herbal potion at their direction. They are amazed—or rather dismayed—that European men demand absolute fidelity from their wives but are not constant themselves, and even some sell their women for money for the pleasure of others. They have, as they see it, much higher standards for themselves—if a marriage does not work, as they see it, why persist, instead of being free to seek a better match."

George observed as Nicolas nodded agreeably. "Your predecessor, Benjamin Franklin, in one of his early publications, *The American Instructor*, provides detailed instructions on herbal abortifacients that women can use to treat a suppression of the courses," complemented Condorcet.[44]

---

44 Farrell, "Ben Franklin."

"Indeed, the herbal recipes used by the Huron in Canada are not very different from the modern ones that are commonly used in our societies today," confirmed Jefferson. He was interrupted by a large noise from the corridor when a waiter tripped only a few paces away from where George stood, crashing with a tray of champagne coupes. George watched as Nicolas supressed a smile, clearly amused at the thought of George behind the wall dealing with the disaster unfolding before him while still keeping his ear alert to the conversation in the room. George stooped down to help the poor chap. When he returned to the conversation, Condorcet was relating Lahontan's observation that Europeans appear to be stronger and more robust until the age of thirty-five, when they weaken, and the Hurons are more resilient. Adario described the delight of Huron women that French men can perform six times in a single night, against only three for the tribesmen, but later in life, the tables turn.

"The Frenchman speaketh," observed Jefferson with mild irritation and then pursued his course diplomatically. "Your compatriot Buffon had made a similar argument about the superiority of the French libido over the American, but please note that Adario's observation is limited to the savages, and does not extend to American citizens, either way."

"And yet Lahontan's writings have had a great influence on the writers of the century, influencing Montesquieu's sense of justice and Rousseau's idea of the noble savage—and Voltaire's *L'Ingénu* was half Huron," rebutted Condorcet, with lighthearted laughter.

A valet strode past George—who admired his balancing skills and gave a curt, approving nod—bearing a tray of mushrooms filled with herbs and creams and interrupting the discussion in the room. He was followed by another with champagne coupes, unhappily accompanied by a whiff of the sweat of his efforts. A mushroom fell on the Persian silk carpet, only to be quickly gobbled by one of Madame Helvétius's cats.

George admired how Jeanne sidestepped the bait from this discussion and navigated back to her interest. "What surprised me most about Lahontan's report on Indian culture is his aversion to property and his affection for liberty," she said delicately. "Ambassador, are these convictions about equality shared in modern America?"

"In an odd way, perhaps to some extent. The principles of liberty and equality are enshrined in our Declaration of Independence, which states that all men are created equal and that they are endowed by their Creator with certain unalienable rights, that among these are life, liberty, and the pursuit of happiness. But where we firmly diverge with the savages is in our commitment to the protection of property. It may well be that the idea of equality comes from the savages, as indeed it may be what has inspired the current French fervour for *égalité* amongst a French elite that lives in great opposition with the idea they entertain."

"Thank you, Monsieur l'Ambassadeur—this is most interesting." Jeanne smiled wryly. "I do note that it is men and not women that are created equal, and that it also implies that slaves are not men."

George was thrilled by Jeanne's composure, standing with her head held high, imperceptibly looking down at Jefferson, who appeared to be as taken by her as George was.

Jefferson continued, "Quite right, *chère Princesse*, that is indeed a subject that concerns me and that I have written about, to great opposition. We are currently in the process of drafting a new constitution, which will hopefully address some of these matters. And if it does not, our children and grandchildren will likely continue to wrestle with them."

Through his window under the portrait of Minette's great-uncle in full battle uniform, George noted that Nicolas left Jeanne the stage, and that he appeared distracted by the presence of a newcomer in the large entrance doors to the salon.

An eternal latecomer, never missing the chance to make a grand entrée, the Chevalier d'Éon stood in the doorway of the room. George recognised him instantly from the painting where d'Éon duelled with the composer Joseph Bologne. He had seen it reproduced in the *Journal*, and had read the sordid story of the two Chevaliers crossing swords, one in a long black dress augmented with prominent red military decorations and an elaborate lace headdress, and the other in elegant beige pantaloons and powdered hair. A gallery of onlookers marvelled at the sight. Stopping slightly longer than strictly warranted, facing the room so that the corners of all eyes had an opportunity to catch sight of her, she strode in. Renowned as a successful general serving the king during the Seven Years' War, and after having spent forty-nine years as a man, he decided in 1777 to forthwith dress as a woman. She claimed to have become a boy only to inherit a fortune. During her exile in London, a betting pool had been started on the stock exchange to wager her true gender—but she had declined to play. Occasionally fighting duels in petticoats, she had quickly learnt to blend in with the extravagant femininity of the time. While d'Éon was not particularly known for her original contributions to the conversation, Minette nevertheless valued her presence for its exoticism, much as for her extensive collection of Japanese vases.[45]

"Benjamin has recently written to me his observations on decomposing human morality into its finite components," Minette announced, her pronunciation of Franklin's name continuing to betray a tribute to the man who had occupied a greater part of her heart than she had wanted to admit. "He is completing his autobiography, and as a natural scientist, he had aimed to identify and isolate the forces that work on the natural world, such as in his famous work on electricity. Now he extends this to morality, identifying thirteen foundational elements: temperance, silence, order, resolution, frugality, industry, sincerity, justice, moderation, cleanliness, tranquillity, chastity, and humility. Each has a precise definition or description. Humility, for example, is simply defined as 'to imitate Jesus and Socrates.'"

"It hardly qualifies as humility to juxtapose the great atheist and the son of God," George heard the abbé quip with feigned indignation.

---

45 Charles-Geneviève-Louis-Auguste-André-Timothée d'Éon de Beaumont (1728–1810), known as the Chevalier d'Éon, was an unusual historic figure. Transgenderism became known for some time in the nineteenth century as eonism.

Minette ignored him and pressed on: "The essential step in this system is a daily practice of self-examination, directing one's attention to each of these aspects."[46]

"Franklin believes morality is composed out of thirteen separable fragments," intervened La Fayette. "Jefferson posits that a garden can be formed by eliminating parts of nature until it is tamed. Tell me, Chevalier, as our American friends appear to be in a dissecting mood, are men and women separate?"

"In brief, no." The Chevalier straightened herself as if addressing her troops. "As many in this room can personally attest, although they will not necessarily admit, they are drawn in various proportions and configurations to both men and women. Those proportions vary greatly from one person to another. Changing identity, as I did, is more unusual, although I believe our friend Condorcet spent the better part of a decade in dresses, and you will all concur it has neither harmed his mind nor his attractive demeanour. One might take the position that men and women are separate, but then they would mix like oil and vinegar, never quite merging. I fear that our century is trying too hard to separate things that should remain connected."

"Interesting idea," murmured Madame Helvétius as she invited the guests to take their seats for dinner "on separate chairs when possible."

---

46 Franklin's autobiography was in fact not published until after 1786, but I am speculating that he perhaps had sent Minette some early thoughts.

The dinner turned the rest of the evening into a tedious event for George, as he could no longer overhear the conversations from his corridor, and his role was reduced to approving nods at the servants speeding by. Many hours later, after all the guests had left, he was allowed to leave and head home under a glowing moonlight. In growing admiration, as he walked through a quiet city, satisfied with his ruse, George rejoiced at the thought of seeing Jeanne the next day and hearing her report on the evening.

9

The Recovery

The note he received by a police courier the following morning instructed George to meet Inspecteur Lenoir at three o'clock in front of the church of Ville d'Avray. The village was on the far side of the Saint-Cloud domain, just west of Paris. Inspecteur Lenoir had given no further details. George could only speculate that the zebra had been found or that they wanted him to witness its recovery. Although irritated by the imperious tone of the note, he had no choice but to go, as the situation needed to be resolved before the representatives of the English queen realised her zebra had gone missing—and there was some appeal in discovering why a stuffed animal had become valuable enough to steal. Learning who the thief was, or possibly, who the police had decided to label as the thief, had its own interest. George was relieved that he clearly was no longer a suspect, nor his staff, which although unlikely, he had not been entirely able to put out of his mind after the initial conversation with Lenoir.

"Did the note bring any good news?" Jeanne ventured, possibly seeing the relief in his expression.

"Possibly. Who knows. It is from Lenoir, and he asks me to come to Ville d'Avray." George sighed. "As usual, he shrouds everything in a mysterious cloud."

Jeanne brightened, taking the note from George's hand and staring at it. "Perhaps he found the zebra? And can I come? I've never been to Avray."

George was startled by her newfound assertiveness. "It could be perilous," he warned. "I have no idea what is going on there, so do you really want to take the risk?"

"Of course! I feel it is a little bit my zebra, and we've also already taken the risk with the Académie to dress me as a man." With an ironic smile she continued. "Now I can act like one."

"Oh, why not—it seems reasonable that you would want to witness the next chapter, and I would enjoy your company."

The carriage that Jeanne had fetched entered the courtyard just after midday. The coachman stood facing the horses, feeding them a handful of hay and mumbling in a guttural regional dialect that George could not discern. A tall man with a bit of hunch on the right side of his back, a sturdy and resigned gaze, dark sideburns that descended to flank his chin before soaring above tobacco-discoloured lips etched by decades of sunburn. Jeanne paid him the price of the journey as he climbed up on the driver's bench. George greeted the man and thanked him for taking them to Ville d'Avray.

"Though how thankful I will really be," George said softly to Jeanne, "is yet to be determined. Who knows what this ride is getting us into. Lenoir is unpredictable."

"Yes," Jeanne replied with a smile, "I myself am very curious. I am mostly concerned about the condition of the zebra, if we even find it."

Emerging from the rue des Saints-Pères, they turned left along the Seine, following it for an hour until they were well outside the city. After a short pause at an auberge, they headed into the gently rising forest road towards Versailles, from which a side path would take them to Ville d'Avray over the next two hours.

Several policemen in dark blue capes stood by the heavily scaffolded church portal. Saint Nicolas in Ville d'Avray had remained incomplete for so long that it scarcely seemed safe to enter anymore.

"They are making sure the holy spirit doesn't escape," somewhat blasphemously quipped George.

"It is probably holding up the building," returned Jeanne, "but I wonder where Lenoir is, having ordered us here—and whether he has our zebra."

"The queen's zebra, but yes."

Lenoir emerged from the church's crudely baroque doors as the carriage slowed to a halt. Jeanne leapt out after the long drive, and George followed with lesser ease.

"Do you know the brothers Robert?" Lenoir asked after he had approached them. He was wearing the same heavy boots as during their last meeting, although now covered with a fine dust.

George frowned in anticipation of another Lenoir lecture. With his spiralling approach, it was likely that Lenoir found intellectual meandering a way to add depth and weight to everyday levity. Painting a wide context and ornamenting it with an evocative story was perhaps his way of keeping the dread of routine policework at bay. George had occasionally stopped by the Roberts' workshop on the place des Victoires, on the way to the north entrance of the Palais-Royal. In a similar set up to his own, their atelier was at the back of a courtyard.

Anne-Jean and Nicolas-Louis Robert made flying machines. Their craft required a combination of skills: the balloons needed the production of vast amounts of hydrogen for buoyancy, as well as workmen with the ability to handle the temperature drop as the gas was released into the envelope. The hydrogen was produced by pouring sulphuric acid on scrap iron and capturing the resulting gas. Weaving sturdy yet lightweight silks for the covering of the airship was particularly difficult. Fortunately, the court had fostered a large silk industry mainly to indulge the whims of Parisian fashion, which could now also be put to a loftier purpose. Flax from Provence allowed the fabrication of solid yet thin ropes to strengthen the silk envelope. Their atelier had separate rooms for each specialty. On the upper floor, George had once been lucky enough to be allowed a peek into a small space dedicated to the scientific instruments that would be carried up to measure the temperature and pressure at various altitudes. He had marvelled how such miracles of modern technology could emerge in buildings that stared back in time.

In 1783, just two years after the very first flight, witnessed by a vast crowd of four hundred thousand, a balloon had risen from the Jardin des Tuileries. Franklin had attended, both with the eye of the scientist and that of the ambassador concerned about facing an airborne force in a future military conflict. A drawback was that the early balloons drifted with the wind, thousands of meters into the clouds, and landed randomly, entirely at the mercy of the elements.

"Yes," George answered, "I know the brothers Robert. Why do you ask?"

In his habit of leaving questions unanswered, Lenoir continued: "The Domaine de Saint-Cloud lies between here and the Seine. Just before the queen pried it from Orléans last year, the Robert brothers had held a demonstration of their newest creation, the dirigible. The King of Sweden was visiting Paris at the time and witnessed it rising above the Grande Cascade from the terrace of the Saint-Cloud palace. The machine had soared above the building towards Meudon. Drifting ever upward, the two men in the basket stuck a bayonet into the belly of the balloon above them. It rapidly deflated and unceremoniously crashed into a nearby pond."

"I recall Ambassador de Staël recounting having attended the ballooning event with his king when we spoke at the unveiling of the zebra in the rue des Saints-Pères."

Unperturbed and not taking the hint, Lenoir continued: "You will appreciate, Monsieur du Paon, the purpose of the new machine. The dirigible is about control of the flight path by the pilot. The earlier balloons were lifted by the wind—or more precisely by the difference in gas densities inside and outside the envelope—and they then drifted with the clouds wherever nature would deem to take them. The only option open to the passengers was to puncture the balloon to hopefully gently nudge it back to the ground."

"Perhaps they should have taken a Bayesian approach?"

"I might come to that." Lenoir's tone betrayed a tinge of irritation at George's teasing taunt. "The dirigible was intended to have man harness the forces of nature to control the flying machine, and not to be a mere subject to their vagaries. As a naturalist, I am sure you can relate to this desire. The early dirigible was equipped with oars, which were soon found to be perfectly useless. The rudder was slightly more useful as it allowed changing direction slightly, combined with the elongated shape of the envelope. The Robert brothers were adapting an idea that Jean Baptiste Meusnier had recently presented at the Académie des sciences—a place you and Jeanne are now familiar with. Meusnier's design called for eighty men to drive three propellers to power the dirigible. Substituting this cohort by three sailors with oars was a bit optimistic."

"I was accompanied by an assistant—you know that women are not admitted into the Académie," interrupted George, weary of the ubiquitous reach of the Parisian police.

"Indeed, I know both of these facts to be true and that they do not contradict anything I have stated," Lenoir continued, lowering his raised left eyebrow. "In any event, what this demonstrates is that it took a mere four years from man's first conquest of the laws of gravity to desiring actual control of the flight path in lieu of drifting with the wind. Not content with sending back Newton's apple from the field where it had naturally landed, the Robert brothers wanted to define where the apple would go next."

"Crashing into a Meudon pond can hardly be described as conquering nature."

"True, but it betrays the desired direction of progress: control through mechanisation."

"As fascinating as it may be, might I ask, Inspecteur Lenoir, why are we meeting you here in Ville d'Avray?" ventured Jeanne.

"Forgive me, Mademoiselle Laplume, or need I say Princess," Lenoir said, raising an amused eyebrow, "I have taken too much of your time already. My men will presently accompany you to the auberge where I have retained two adjacent rooms for you. Forgive the somewhat rustic accommodation, but it was the only option for our purpose. The owner, Pierre Lacroix, is an old acquaintance of mine from very different circumstances, which guarantees that he is deeply in my debt and will do everything in his power to make your rest comfortable, serve his best wine for dinner, and see that you are safe and rested by morning. I might suggest you retire early, as I propose to pick you up at five o'clock, accompanied by six of my men."

As Lenoir drove off with his men, Jeanne burst out, "Why did he call me Princess? Was he at Madame Helvétius's? How can he know? This man is nothing short of creepy."

George laughed heartedly. "He would reply that it is his business to know," George answered. "But honestly, I have no idea how he finds out all these things. Very few people knew about our masquerade. Let's see . . . Nicolas, his sister, Mathilde, and the two of us. And I am confident none of them would speak to the police. But I would not be worried. He seems well-intentioned. Mostly. Although one can never tell."

"That is not very comforting," Jeanne huffed. "In my circles, everyone is terrified of the police! And the way he spoke about the owner of our auberge is hardly reassuring."

"Understandable—although, ironically, your circles are no longer the same. You appear to have conquered the American ambassador for one." George tried to comfort her. "Now, the travel has tired me, and I would love to enjoy some of that good wine that Lenoir's machinations will provide us!"

•

George had admonished the innkeeper to awaken them in time. The next morning, as promised, Lacroix knocked on George's door, announcing a meal of hot milk, bread, and eggs for him and Jeanne. While they ate, Lenoir was waiting outside in a fiacre. Through the condensation on the dining room window, they could glimpse its polished black surface reflecting the light of the torches of the six policemen on horseback.

Jeanne ate hurriedly, repeatedly looking up from her plate to glance through the window at the awaiting carriage.

"Do please hurry," Jeanne urged George.

"But you've hardly touched your eggs," George said, pointing at Jeanne's plate.

"I'm too excited to eat," Jeanne said, getting to her feet.

George managed two more bites before hurrying after Jeanne.

George and Jeanne, nodding to the policeman who held the door to the carriage, got in quickly and settled on the hard leather benches. Unusually, Lenoir greeted them in silence, and Jeanne gave George a quiet look of surprise. With two men riding in front and four behind the carriage, the caravan left the village square, passed a few farmhouses lining the road through the now barren wheat fields, and soon reached the edge of the forest.

Although it was a clear night, the darkness required them to move slowly; the autumn foliage dampened the glow from the half-moon enough that the leading horsemen struggled to discern obstacles on the road. It had been raining during the night and the fallen wet leaves covering the ground dampened the sound of the hooves. The wooden cart wheels crackled from the crushing of acorns as the group dove deeper into the woods. The road's irregular rhythm gradually seduced the passengers into picking up their night's slumber—George was the last to resign himself to sleep.

A particularly thick branch jolted the carriage, catapulting the company from their seats and firmly landing them into the new day.

Lenoir opened the joust: "Do you subscribe to individuality, Mademoiselle Laplume?"

"It seems to me that individuals have limited control over their lives," Jeanne replied while supressing a yawn, still sleepy and less accustomed to the culture of the spirited exchange that was the foundation of one's social position, although George could only assume that her induction as a princess had familiarised her somewhat with the custom.

Lenoir continued gently, "I concur, mademoiselle. Our lives are strongly led by the circumstances of our birth and the vagaries of our lives. But the intent of my question was slightly different: do you believe that my officers who accompany us are disjunct individuals, who are separate from their horses and from the trees we are passing and from the air we are breathing? Do all these exist independently?"

George listened with amusement and in wonderment as to where Lenoir's meanders would lead them, but also feeling a twinge of remorse that he had perhaps not explored Jeanne's mind quite enough. Or perhaps his sense of responsibility and natural timidity had led him to sidestep a more intimate liaison.

Jeanne smiled amicably. "I am not sure how you mean this. There are six policemen, thousands of trees, and much air."

"Fair enough, but if we were to remove the air, would the policemen and the trees remain?"

"That seems like an absurd idea, but I suppose they would not."

"All right, now that we have established that the trees, the policemen, and the air are connected, what about the trees themselves. Do they exist independently from each other?"

At this, Jeanne perked up, straightening in her seat. "Whenever I make drawings of trees, I am struck by how their crowns complement each other, how they appear to mingle and form a single virtual shape. Their roots interweave as together and in competition they seek water and nourishment. The oak trees drop their acorns onto the same forest floor, and their saplings reach for the same sunlight. So at the very least you can say that they are a close family, perhaps something more?"

"Very good," Lenoir said, nodding with enthusiasm. "Such is the fabric of nature, woven like a Persian silk rug with thousands of knots and patterns under every thumb-sized segment." Slightly raising an eyebrow, he added, "Such as those at Madame Helvétius's salon."

George and Jeanne exchanged a worried glance.

Seemingly satisfied with the effect on his audience, Lenoir continued: "Mademoiselle Laplume, what is your view on my six agents outside? If they are part of nature, they, too, might be deeply connected—or perhaps you consider that they are not part of nature? Are they machines, like a clock, or perhaps another category altogether? Having breathed a semblance of life into many dead animals, notably a royal zebra that is our concern today, I am confident you have a view on this."

"Your agents are precisely six, not more, not fewer."

"Very well," he replied. Turning to George, he asked, "Are you familiar with the Phrygian cap, or pileus, if you wish?"

George was now firmly out of his morning slump and felt himself being dragged into a new twist in the conversation. He was aware of the pileus mushrooms that grew widely in the woods in the area, and of their unique properties: thin white stems with a red-brownish cap, appearing quickly in small clusters in the autumn, and which were reminiscent of Phrygian hats. In his evenings at the Palais-Royal, George had picked up the rumblings from some of the more extreme political activists advocating the king's overthrow and who were starting to adopt this hat as a symbol of their struggle. He assumed that Lenoir was surely aware of this. The mushrooms circulated in the Palais-Royal in certain cafés, but Nicolas had described how they were consumed at soupers as an alternative to the laudanum that some preferred. The laudanum, however, appeared to lead to an increasing dependence, in contrast to pileus. Reputedly, the clergy used pileus to deepen meditation and religious experience in some convents. George had never had the opportunity to experiment but had often been curious about its effect.

"Would you be alluding to the experiential extremists or the political ones?" retorted George.

"Mushroom—not regicide indeed." Seeing Jeanne in wide-eyed wonderment at the exchange, Lenoir was eager to enlighten her, and George did his best to avoid rolling an eye. "Forgive me, Mademoiselle Laplume, and allow me to explain. Pileus is a mushroom with the curious ability to transform one's perception of the world around us. Consumption, even in mild quantities, allows mystics to see mystery; revolutionaries, revolution; botanists, the fabric of nature—and perhaps even naturalists, the essence of an animal."

"Does that imply that you see whatever is already in your mind and that your perception simply follows your imagination?" Jeanne asked. "What purpose would that serve? Or do you see something that was not in your mind previously? Do you see inward or outward? And how is this related to the beginning of our conversation?"

Lenoir raised an admiring eyebrow. "All good questions, Mademoiselle Laplume. Those who consume pileus believe they see more sharply that which they wish to observe. There is choice of subject but not of intensity. Nuns will experience more deeply their faith, in the hypothesis that this is where their interest lies. Those who observe nature will see most intensely what you have so eloquently described when you draw trees. The same excellent eye, no doubt, that led to the success of the rendering of the queen's zebra."

George's pride at Jeanne's recognition blended with a mild indignation at being cast aside by the policeman in his role as the master of the workshop.

"The common factor, in any case, is those connections that could not be perceived through everyday senses becoming inescapable. It is undecidable whether this is real, but there is no doubt that the experience is common for most people," continued Lenoir.

George noticed they were taking a path that followed the perimeter of the Saint-Cloud domain. Queen Marie Antoinette had just purchased Saint-Cloud the previous year, after long negotiations with her brother-in-law Orléans, who was eternally in need of cash for the continued development of the Palais-Royal—as well as to fund his lavish and libertine habits. Unusually for royal properties, she had insisted that it be labelled as the Queen's Property and dressed the guards and the valets in her own uniforms. The queen had her own livery, in the same colours as the king's; however, they were mirrored so that the main fabric was red and the braids blue. The reason for the length of the journey was to avoid crossing through the Saint-Cloud property and having to negotiate a passage with the queen's guard.

"So, if I were to digest your mushrooms, I would see how your six policemen are connected?"

"Excellent, Mademoiselle Laplume, except that they are not my mushrooms but those of Monsieur le Comte de Beaubourg. If you had an interest in the connection between my men, and observed them accordingly, you might see that they are from the same family: three are brothers and the three others their cousins. You might also see how their training has welded them into a coherent unit, where each is willing to risk their life for the others. They share a desire for order in society and they love their king, more than their beer. While you may now know these things, you would then also see them."

George was surprised at the appearance of Beaubourg in the conversation. He had last encountered him at the presentation of the zebra at the Académie. He recalled his extraordinary plea to keep the zebra in France, as returning it to England would give that nation some imagined strategic advantage over France by somehow giving it a scientific edge. Earlier, when he had encountered him in the company of Madame du Barry at the Café de Foy, he had been struck by the aggrieved undertone in his defence of exemplary punishment. The connection between Beaubourg, mushrooms, the Roberts' flying machine, and the queen's zebra eluded him, but his admiration grew for Lenoir's ability to paint a tableau of connections and conjectures.

As the carriage continued to make its way down the forest path, still slowed by darkness and the uneven terrain, Lenoir straightened slightly, clearly delighted at how he had enthralled his small audience.

"Allow me to explain Beaubourg's role in all of this," Lenoir said. "Beaubourg owned a set of barns on the far side of the Saint-Cloud property that we are just navigating around. These forests were particularly rich in pileus mushrooms. Beaubourg's men have found a way to farm them and dry them on long screens made from birch so that their hallucinogenic properties were retained. Through his connections, Beaubourg has become a reliable supplier of dried pileus to some of the leading aristocratic houses in Paris, and the bright netherworld of the Palais-Royal, as well as several convents in the surroundings. The court at Versailles under the dour Louis XVI frowned on its use, but Marie Antoinette on her own premises at Saint-Cloud is less constrained. Some of the production has made its way as far as London and Amsterdam. It has become a way for Beaubourg to rebuild some of the family fortune that he had gambled away."

"Was he just trading pileus, or was he also interested in its effects for himself?" wondered George aloud.

"He was actually an avid consumer himself. In fact, it had convinced Beaubourg of the value of going beyond direct observation and fed his suspicion of the scientists at the Académie. He had been particularly struck when your zebra appeared to offer direct insights into the fabric of nature, albeit without assistance of pileus, and became convinced it offered a potentially powerful gateway of perception."

"Your hypothesis is that Beaubourg stole the zebra and is holding it in his pileus barn?" concluded Jeanne.

"This was indeed my strong conviction, and some of my men have scouted the property over the past week to ascertain themselves of the zebra's presence. French agents in Prussia and Saxony had reported through the invisible web of informers that my colleagues and I have built throughout Europe, that those courts had already been approached for their interest in purchasing the English queen's zebra."

"It seems that Beaubourg's focus on money clearly exceeded his interest in how one perceives reality," observed George.

"Indeed, but the buyers' consideration was likely motivated more by an opportunity to embarrass the English Court than by Beaubourg's promise of a keyhole into nature's dynamics. Nevertheless, the urgency of those reports had prompted me to intervene earlier than I had intended, and combined with Beaubourg's presence, this had triggered today's raid and your presence in this carriage so early in the morning."

At George's question whether he was also wanted for producing the pileus extract, Lenoir laughed heartily. "Of course not—that is perfectly legal. It is entirely natural. The only reason one would outlaw the use of a substance that has no known lethal dose or even addictive properties, would be if it became a threat to public order because the citizenry acquired deeper insights than the state. This is highly unlikely, as the production is expensive, and only the aristocracy and the church have easy access to it. Broadening the mind of nuns and counts is harmless, but stealing the property of the English queen has the potential to destabilise our relations, which balance on a knife-edge at the best of times. As you know, we have so far been able to keep the disappearance of the zebra hidden from the British ambassador, and we fully intend to restore it to its rightful place in the rue des Saints-Pères before they become aware it was missing."

George wondered whether Lenoir's chauvinism was not affecting his habitual perspicacity, as surely the British had able spies of their own and would have been informed about the zebra's theft. But perhaps Lenoir knew through his spies that their spies did not know. Or perhaps there was merely an unspoken agreement between spies to pretend that other spies did not know.

The carriage had come to a halt, and Lenoir excused himself to confer briefly with his men. The dimness of the night was making way for a distant shimmer of sunlight through the tree cover, which had started to erase the straggling stars. Lenoir's men had extinguished their torches, and the muffled sound of powder being firmly pounded into the bottom of gun barrels could be heard outside. Reappearing at the window of the fiacre, Lenoir instructed his passengers to wait for his return, as it was too dangerous to join his men until they had secured the barn, only fifteen minutes farther by foot.

"A single armed policeman will stay with you," Lenoir assured them. "The coachman is also armed as well as an excellent shooter. I did not expect any danger, and still do not, but am merely acting out of an abundance of prudence."

George could not help but worry, and saw that Jeanne was equally uneasy about their situation. To distract her, as Lenoir and his men faded into the forest, George asked Jeanne her view on the events so far. She looked pale and tired—both of them had risen early in the day, and George wondered whether being quartered between social classes was taking a toll on her and her vulnerability.

But she surprised George by dismissing her fatigue and apprehension, allowing her curiosity to prevail. Or perhaps she was trying to distract and comfort him. "Lenoir knows how to blend amusement, education, and action into a compelling story!" she said cheerfully. "I will be enormously relieved when we recover the zebra and when it's on its way back to London. I do wonder, though, about the pileus and whether it could be helpful for our work."

"Indeed, a strange story, but how might the pileus help you?"

"If Beaubourg is correct that our zebra provided a similar insight as pileus might, would not our work on future projects be enhanced if we could use it to better understand the essence of an animal? Imagine how it might help with the upcoming beasts that Ambassador Jefferson has offered the Comte de Buffon? With perhaps a better understanding of the forces of nature that have shaped them, we could express the majesty of American wilderness through the beasts."

"I see—although I rather wonder whether Buffon doesn't want us to do the exact opposite just to embarrass the Americans."

"That would not be ethical. We are scientists and not politicians."

"You are right, it might not. Although we should always evaluate the ethics of any situation, it is more rare that we have the freedom to act on them. In any case, if all goes well today, we can see with Lenoir whether we might divert a small supply of pileus for the workshop."

Their wait stretched for over an hour as the day continued to brighten. They listened for gunshots in the distance. The sounds of the awakening forest surrounded them, as birds twirped with steadily increasing raucousness, treetops rustled, and the underbrush occasionally betrayed the first furtive food dash of the day. Suddenly the voices of Lenoir and two of his men emerged from the background. From their loud tone, George inferred that their mission had been successful, and they rushed out to interrogate them.

"All went well," Lenoir assured them. "Beaubourg and eight of his collaborators have been apprehended and are currently being held under armed guard, waiting for our return. Most importantly, the zebra is safe, although already in a crate readied for transportation, confirming my fear that it might have slipped away to a foreign court if we had not intervened in a timely way."

Gathering the horses that had been left behind, they set course for the barn ahead. "I could not help but ask Beaubourg whether he thought he should be punished according to his own views, favouring exemplary over proportional justice," Lenoir gently boasted on the way to the barn.

"Indeed," George responded, recalling his evening witnessing Beaubourg in the Café de Foy, "did he have the intellectual consistency to agree?"

"He just let out an aristocratic grunt!" triumphantly exclaimed the policeman.

The large barn doors were open, and the captured men were lying bound on the ground. In deference to his status, Beaubourg remained unshackled, as he had given his word that he would comply with any requests. He greeted the new visitors with the courteous habits engrained through generations, but with a blank stare, mixing haughtiness with resignation. Lenoir's men had opened the crate of the zebra. Jeanne and George went into the barn and were struck by long shelves of wooden racks lining one side covered with a brown substance. Underneath, an elaborate system of porous pipes delivered dry air from a wood furnace at the far end. A cupboard held rows of small bright red boxes, presumably containing the dried pileus.

George exhaled a breath he had not realised he had been holding—it was readily apparent that the zebra had been crated with care and was wholly undamaged, to the great relief of all. But Beaubourg had confirmed that, had it not been for Lenoir's intervention, it was going to be sent to Saxony the following week through the mediation of Princess Maria Cunegonda of Saxony. In addition to being the monarch of the Thorn and Essen convent school statelets that groomed and delivered brides from the highest German aristocratic families into the great French houses, she also represented the interests of the Saxon court, as she was well connected in France. The princess was the aunt of Louis XVI and the lover of some of the wealthiest women in European nobility.[47] In addition to her own high rank in German nobility, this sapphic aristocratic web gave her access to the French network, through which Beaubourg had offered her the zebra.

Saxony would be disappointed to lose this small element of leverage over England, which it could have used in defending its position in the waltz of Central European power politics.

The crate with the zebra was sealed again and loaded onto a heavy cart, and the company set out for Paris, escorted by two policemen. The others remained behind to transfer the prisoners to common prison and Beaubourg to the Bastille.

---

47 The princess was the lover of Madame de Brionne, the widow since 1761 of the very rich Duc de Brionne and reputed to be the most beautiful woman in France. Madame de Brionne's other lover was the Duc de Choiseul, the Minister of Foreign Affairs. After her husband's death, she convinced Louis XV to appoint her the stable master at Versailles, keeping the position warm for her son. Uniquely, she became the second most powerful person at the Versailles court, managing five hundred staff and a thousand horses. The irresistible Madame Brionne had met Princess Cunegonda in Spa in the summer of 1771, and they became lovers for a summer and friends for life. Cunegonda later had a liaison with Madame Folard, the wife of Hubert de Folard—at the time the French ambassador in Munich. Source: Welten, 2019.

"I am relieved that the queen's zebra will be back in our custody soon. The British ambassador is due to inspect any day, as well as pay us for our work," George said with a loud sigh. Looking sideways at Jeanne, he teased her, "But it seems you are mostly wondering about a red box journey?"

Jeanne was clutching a basket containing twenty small red cardboard boxes, protecting them from being projected by the shock of a protruding root on the road.

10

A Platypus

Several days after their return from Ville d'Avray, having recovered the queen's zebra, George and his staff were preparing for a final visit from the British ambassador. The weather had grown increasingly grey and wet as autumn firmly settled in. A fire simmering from the early morning was starting to warm the atelier.

"Let us receive the ambassador with due honour. And please, please don't breathe a word about the misadventures of our zebra," George admonished his collaborators.

"Of course, of course." Jeanne nodded. "I wouldn't dream of it."

"Not a word," added Gaston, crossing himself.

"It is such a relief that this tale had a happy ending," continued George with a growing frown. He stood up from the decorated oak chair and paced about the room. "There is a small disappointment I must share with you both, a commission I had hoped we would obtain. Perhaps you overheard the story from the Comte de Buffon at our unveiling? Or maybe it was elsewhere," he added, momentarily doubting his memory, dazed from the roller-coaster of emotions of the days past.

"Another zebra?" ventured Jeanne.

"Actually, no. Buffon told us that he had wagered with the American ambassador that animals in France are bigger than in America. Not letting the sleight pass, Jefferson had commissioned a military friend of his to hunt for giant beasts. The result apparently was a giant grizzly bear, a daunting moose, and a towering elk. The skins of the animals had arrived in Paris, and naturally I hoped that the commission to naturalise them would be granted to us. No such luck, however."

"I remember the story," said Jeanne. "Did Monsieur le Comte send them elsewhere because of what happened to our zebra?"

"No, no, I don't even think Buffon was ever aware of its misplacement, but it became a political matter. In fact, the success of the zebra may have worked against us, because Buffon wanted to avoid the animals looking too impressive. The commission went to Deyrolle, who are of course competent colleagues but, as you know, much more conventional in their work and less focussed on what nature aims to tell us through its creatures. In general, Deyrolle produces a flow of specimens with little expression to recommend them."[48]

---

48 In actuality, Deyrolle was not founded until 1831.

"A shame. Animals from such unfamiliar forests would have been a wonderful way to experiment with our new design process through the pileus."

"Pileus?" Gaston asked Jeanne. "What is pileus? A new winery?"

"In a sense," explained George, "in some sense, Gaston." Turning to Jeanne and momentarily silent as he observed her, he explained: "Actually, this commission was more a question of international diplomacy than a naturalist's quest, and Buffon was not the man to retreat from his claim to the American ambassador of the superiority of Europe's nature, even if it meant doctoring the evidence offered."

They were interrupted by the muffled sound of a four-wheeled carriage pulling up to the gate. The large gates in the rue des Saints-Pères were opened to allow the British carriage to enter, past the two policemen that Lenoir had insisted be posted in the courtyard around the clock. John Sackville, Third Duke of Dorset—the guest the carriage harboured—had only been the British representative in Paris for two years, but he had done justice to his reputation at Vauxhall Gardens, and George had glimpsed him more than once at the Palais-Royal, indulging in the attractions of his fresh diplomatic posting.

Dorset looked every part the military man he had been, stepping down onto the granite pavement, rod straight in a bright red coat, sabre dangling by his side, radiating the discrete professional optimism of a diplomat. He turned around to assist his far younger companion in a white silk dress lined with rows of sky-blue ribbons, brown hair cascading in curls from her bonnet, her white shoes decorated with a row of pearls, their delicate soles meeting the granite of the courtyard moments after the ambassador. George had heard that he had brought with him from London a Venetian ballerina, who had been the principal dancer at the King's Theatre at Haymarket. He was so enthralled with her that Thomas Gainsborough eternalised her in 1782, at Dorset's request. The picture had been exhibited a few years earlier at a Paris salon that George had attended, and his memory not failing him, he instantly recognised the girl.

"It is my pleasure to welcome Your Excellency and mademoiselle to our humble workshop," said George, bowing his head deeply.

"Forgive me, this is Giovanna Baccelli," clarified the ambassador. The ballerina, used to being mostly banned from the conversation by the duke, feigned an air of amused indifference.

"A pleasure, mademoiselle," George said, taking her hand in his and bowing slightly. "May I introduce my collaborators Jeanne Laplume and Gaston? They are largely responsible for the work you are about to see."

George invited the pair to enter the workshop where Jeanne and Gaston had set up the zebra to be favourably displayed. George introduced his collaborators to the ambassador and his ballerina.

With unfailing British delight at its most exuberant, Dorset proceeded to ensure the staff of the atelier that Her Majesty would be most pleased with the final pose her zebra had assumed, or rather, that had been assumed for it.

Dorset spoke a passable French and immediately proceeded to utter his own personal admiration for the result. "It is splendid work indeed, splendid, most extraordinary—Her Majesty will be delighted. One fears being trampled upon by this beast with its strong musculature, its wild gaze, and recalcitrant pose. Excellent. Excellent," continued to expound the duke, dropping any of the reticence and implied irony that a Frenchman might have maintained. "So you are the man I've heard so much about. The skin arranger, as it were, from the Greek *taxis* 'to order' and *derma* 'skin.' We should perhaps call your profession taxidermy.[49] A great word for it, in my opinion. A fine profession indeed. Reviving the ancient Egyptian skill, serving Osiris, of course."

"It was an honour, Your Excellency," muttered George, baffled by his barrage of bland blather.

Dorset gave the zebra a more critical look, and his tone softened. "I am also particularly pleased at avoiding the large expenditure to compensate the Princess of Saxony and am thankful to the good work of the Paris police. We are here today to see it off to London!"

George stood momentarily dumbfounded. "My profuse apologies, Your Excellency, since the object was safely back in my hands, I did not want to trouble you with the tale of its escape. But it seems you were aware all along," stuttered George, embarrassed at appearing to have intended to deceive the British envoy.

"Not at all, my good man. Splendid adventure, splendid. We

---

49 The word taxidermist was not in use until the beginning of the nineteenth century, introduced in the *Nouveau dictionnaire d'histoire naturelle* by Louis Dufresne (1803).

keep a close eye on Saxony and have good agents there. So important as a buffer between Prussia and Austria. Need to watch it carefully. Essential to avoid being drawn into another European conflict not of our choosing. Maintain some balance. Anyway, we picked up the trace of your wild escapee and we were well informed of the negotiations between Beaubourg and Saxony. Untameable by man, indeed, only by God!"

"I assure you of my profound regret and I wish I had been able to avoid these circumstances, but for our artistry to become a matter of state was the furthest from my expectations."

"Yes, yes, yes," confirmed Dorset impatiently. "Presently, the payment for your work has already been deposited with the Caisse d'amortissement in the rue Vivienne, as you instructed."

His bank had been established a decade earlier in the rue Vivienne. During the crisis of 1783, a run on the bank was deflected when Talleyrand had intervened and forced an augmentation of the capital, to a leverage ratio of at least one-third. This was widely considered the absolute minimum for stable financial institutions. A Franco-British trade treaty had just been concluded and the vast sums that the French treasury continued to require to finance the debt contracts to support the American independence war provided openings for excellent returns. Speculation was rife—but access to the right information before it became public was critical.

Nicolas participated occasionally in the Bellechase group, which included de Talleyrand, Panchaud, Dupont de Nemours, and others. They shared a Dutch banker, which allowed them to tap into its efficient financial system. George was not wealthy by any measure compared to the vast fortunes of the aristocracy, but his access to their sources of advance information through his friend Nicolas had vastly increased his capital. The new treaty with the British would allow him to soon invest the generous reward from the British Crown for the zebra. Being connected to such deeply self-interested protectors substantially reduced the risk to George's savings.

Jeanne had remained silent, but with the genuine enthusiasm that sometimes allows spontaneity to thread the needle of protocol, she asked the duke to satisfy her extreme curiosity as to the unlikely animal he had alluded to.

George shot her a concerned glance, but the ambassador was charmed by Jeanne and seized the opportunity to move on from the stiff and rather tedious apologies of the taxidermist. "There was no doubt in my mind, and indeed in the British mind, if I can speak of the greatest of nations that I represent, there was no doubt the work would be excellent," Dorset continued to pontificate. "In fact, I have undertaken to secure a commission for another most unlikely animal."

Dorset called for his valet to bring in a rolled-up drawing, which he proceeded to unfurl on the oak table of the atelier. It represented an odd creature, as if a beaver and a duck had been fused. The long brown furry body was shown swimming in water, somewhat darker on its back than its underside, with short-clawed paws connected by membranes, and a split tail, but one was mainly struck by its head: the small skull that one might expect on a rodent was ornamented by a sizeable rubbery duck's bill. The bottom right hand of the drawing showed the name of the artist, F. P. Nodder.[50]

"What is this animal? Is it real?" exclaimed Jeanne.

The duke smiled mischievously. George could see he was clearly satisfied with the effect the drawing had on his small audience. After a tense moment of silence, the duke then proceeded to explain that it was an animal native of Van Diemen's Land, a large island to the south of Australia, originally discovered by the Dutchman Abel Tasman and prudently named to honour his superior instead of himself. The governor of Australia had recently sent back a salted and preserved specimen to the Royal Society in London, who now wished to have it reconstructed by the finest artisan in Europe.

George stifled a sigh of relief—he took the commission as a sign that Britain did not hold a grudge over the temporary escape of the queen's zebra and thanked the ambassador. Exploring the essence of the platypus's shape and expressions would be a grand challenge. Having assured him that the skin would be soon delivered and having settled upon a price, the ambassador took his leave and, with his ballerina, promptly departed under the stern gaze of the posted Paris policemen.

"All ends well in the best of worlds," George quoted. "I am so relieved that we have completed this work—and will be

50 The actual drawing was reproduced in the *Naturalist's Miscellany* in 1799, thirteen years later than our story. Source: "Platypus," Wikipedia.

even more relieved when the crated beast is in the belly of an England-bound ship."

Jeanne, however, was already thinking of the platypus. "What an amazing animal!" she exclaimed. "Clearly too small to be American. How do we find more drawings of this one? How does it run? Does it crawl, waddle, or swim? Does it stand upright or just crawl?"

"A creepy lizard, if you asked me." Gaston shrugged, triggering a shared eruption of laughter and relief.

A different outcome would have doomed the business or its owner. The felicitous ending of the turbulent zebra affair was enough grounds for celebration, and George wanted to offer Jeanne and Gaston something unusual. Most of the restaurants with forks were reserved for the wealthy aristocracy, and neither George nor most certainly his staff would be welcomed. La Bouteille d'Or across from the Notre Dame cathedral had been a tavern since 1631, and had now evolved into a restaurant with forks, but one welcoming a diverse clientele. With Jeanne's training as a princess, she would fit right in, but for Gaston, it would be a slightly daunting experience. He would also need to overcome the effeminate reputation forks had amongst workers.

The autumn weather was cloudy but free of rain, and they walked the twenty minutes to the cathedral. Gaston's soft whistling was a good sign. The façade of the cathedral towered across from the entrance to the restaurant, its menacing gargoyles poised to redirect any rainwater away from the delicate gothic ornamentation.

Although he didn't think of himself as particularly religious, George was always particularly touched by the sweeping rosettes of stained glass in the transepts and over the main gate. Twenty-four rays in three concentric circles represented the twelve tribes of Israel and the twelve signs of the zodiac, in a Pythagorean explosion of blue and red glass segments. Like the mandalas he was familiar with from exploring the manuscripts of the Bibliothèque nationale in the rue des Petits Champs, the rosettes expressed the unity and wholeness, the relationship between the sum and the parts.

His eyes adjusting to the darkness after crossing the threshold of the tavern, George identified a small table tucked away beneath the wooden shaft of the staircase leading to the next floor. Being out of the limelight would make his guests feel comfortable, and it was also consistent with his own modest origins. Due to the early hour, there were few other patrons. He marvelled at how comfortable Jeanne appeared to be, exploring every detail of the space with her eyes, unperturbed by the unfamiliarity, drawn by the new. Gaston would clearly require the administration of a couple of glasses of claret to settle in. Having agreed to the suggestion of their table attendant, he proceeded to administer the medicine, raising a glass to their joint success.

"You have both suffered the inside of a police cell, Jeanne discovered the inside of the Académie des sciences and the forests of Saint-Cloud, and I had to endure the torturous twists of Inspecteur Lenoir's tales. Ironically, it was the quality of the work that led to all of this. Never regret. Good work matters." George delivered his speech. "I want to thank you both."

After an egg with mayonnaise, a sturdy beef stew, a serving of a rare Peruvian root vegetable which was being aggressively promoted by the court to sidestep another devastating famine as seven years prior, and sustained gulps of wine, Gaston's tongue loosened.

"What is this spongy thing on my plate?" he asked, poking at it.

"It is called a potato. It was taken in the southern Americas and brought back by our explorers," explained George. "Our friend the Comte de Buffon is hoping that it can replace bread and avoid food shortages in the future. He hopes it is embraced by the people."

"What? Never. Instead of bread, this? Not in my lifetime." Gaston wrinkled his nose. "Even when I was imprisoned, they gave me bread. As they should."

"You were in prison?" enquired Jeanne, with a frisson of excitement. George looked over to see her enthralled, likely imagining a sordid unknown past for her colleague.

"Just like you," deadpanned Gaston, "when the inspecteur took us for interrogation. They tried to intimidate me. Talking loudly, almost shouting, confusing me with complicated questions. But no. I held firm. I just imagined the wine my brother would serve me next time we were together. I just whistled."

George laughed heartily. "It helped that you had nothing to hide, but I am sure you were both courageous. The police don't have a great reputation in this matter, but I think they never really suspected you and were just taking every precaution."

Unperturbed, Gaston described how whistling various tunes in different occasions helped him cope. During his arrest, he had reached back to a melody of his childhood.

George listened intently, smiling gently, while Jeanne appeared more remotely lost in thought.

11

Saint-Georges

At the unveiling of the zebra, George recalled observing that the music had appeared to enthral his assistant. Jeanne quite obviously had not heard much modern music, particularly as complex as that of Bologne's first sonata. Perhaps his impression had been merely an illusion, swept up in the tension of her work being judged by the assembled audience. Jeanne continued to impress him, and he kept musing about how he might help her further.

He considered and rejected the thought that he was perhaps too preoccupied with his assistant. The salon scenes in the elegant green dress remained etched in his mind, sharpened by his odd vantage point during the evening. He had retained two entrances for Thursday afternoon, when Bologne was holding one of his regular subscription concerts, during which he played more popular kinds of music. Jeanne's surprise when he asked her to join him soon dissolved into excitement at the opportunity to taste another domain of society.

"Are you ready, Jeanne? We must leave soon!" he called out to the other room in the apartment—the room that had been Violette's.

"Does this blue suit me?" she asked lightheartedly, appearing in the door opening in a light blue satin cotton dress, offset with white ribbons. George briefly stiffened, as he recalled the last time Violette wore it. They had gone for an afternoon stroll along the Seine. The weather had been brisk, but sunny. Three, perhaps four years ago.

"It does!" he forced himself to exclaim, ignoring a fleeting thought that Jeanne might grow into Violette's role.

It had been out of the question that she would wear the green silk dress from her evening at Madame Helvétius. Others might identify it and reveal the masquerade. The dress was also well beyond the stature of the companion of a naturalist, even a successful and increasingly famous one, but a bourgeois nonetheless. George had asked Jacques to retrieve the blue dress from the attic trunk where Violette's clothes were stored, and it had fit her well. The two women shared a waistline, although Jeanne's bust clearly required restraining with greater force. It struck him how much younger Jeanne was.

Heading out across the Seine through the gardens of the Tuileries palace to the Palais-Royal, George took the opportunity to hold her arm to steady her balance, as she was not used to walking in tight, fashionable shoes. Entering from the rue de

Richelieu, they walked down the colonnade to the concert hall, where a line had already formed.

An elegant man in a silver coat broke from the crowd and took a few steps in their direction, and tentatively stated, "Monsieur du Paon, I believe?"

"Most certainly. To whom do I have the honour?"

"Forgive my temerity, Monsieur du Paon. I am the Comte d'Ogny. I have the pleasure of being the Grand Master of the loge of the Société Olympique. We have not been introduced, but you are famous of course as the tamer of the English queen's zebra. It is the talk of the town and has led to much debate amongst our members." D'Ogny paused, looking to Jeanne. "And who is your most elegant companion?" he asked, approvingly taking off his hat in salutation.

"Forgive me, Comte. This is Jeanne Madelin, a long-time friend." George was disturbed that the presence of the zebra in Paris had become such common knowledge, although he knew that intrigue and rumour echoed quickly through the colonnades of the Palais-Royal.

Although they had agreed upon this appellation, Jeanne seemed to be at the same time excited at hearing herself described as a friend and disturbed at having to change name once more. The complex emotions played upon her face, and he realised that he had come to know this young woman so well. And George speculated from d'Ogny's raised eyebrow and close scrutiny of his companion, that the comte was wondering why such a young and beautiful courtesan might not aim higher than a mere naturalist.

Jeanne interrupted his thought, picking up the style of direct questioning that she had deployed with apparent success at the evening in Madame Helvétius's salon. "Monsieur le Comte, if I may ask, what is the Société Olympique?"

George knew that this closed and secretive Freemason loge had been founded four years earlier by two music lovers, Charles-Marin de La Haye des Fosses and Claude-François Rigoley d'Ogny. They had secured a lavish building at number sixty-five in the Palais-Royal across from the rue de Richelieu entrance, where Jeanne and he had just entered. In their new premises, concerts were held, accessible only to their three hundred or so members. Such Freemason loges were a chance for social classes to mix, with members from the aristocracy mingling with the bourgeoisie and artists, leading to free-flowing debate on how ideas from the Enlightenment might change the world. Their orchestra was reputed to be excellent. It was constituted of professional musicians and practiced amateur members of the Société. The director of its predecessor institution, the Concert des Amateurs, which had folded in 1780, had been retained. Thus their music director, Josef de Bologne, Chevalier de Saint-Georges, had become the only dark-skinned Freemason in Paris.

"Of course, Mademoiselle Madelin, allow me to explain," responded d'Orgny. "The Société Olympique is a place that allows me to play the cello together with some excellent musicians, many far more talented than I am. Most notably, the Chevalier de Saint-Georges, who leads our orchestra, and whom you will of course have the pleasure of hearing today.

Music gives me great joy. I also have the honour of organising things for the members."

"The Grand Master of a loge is an organiser?"

D'Orgny laughed heartily at Jeanne's directness, but also her perspicacity. "Indeed, my *chère* mademoiselle, the Grand Master organises things. We are a little ridiculous, because we always play dressed in the grandest style, with powdered hair and our most elegant coats, as our Queen Marie Antoinette is not only a great music lover, but she has adopted the distressing habit of joining us unannounced. So now we must be prepared during every concert for a royal visit."

"That seems a little inconvenient," observed George with a frown, "but I suppose it is unavoidable. And the Chevalier de Saint-Georges selects the music and trains the orchestra?"

"Indeed. Last year, I asked him to commission a new piece by this very popular German composer, Monsieur Haydn. Bologne is himself a great innovator in music—he brought us a new form, the symphonie concertante, really a quintessentially French form. Instead of just focussing on musical harmony like the Germans so tediously do, it features two soloists as it were competing with each other and with the orchestra. It is a kind of duel, which much appealed to Bologne's other passion—as an outstanding swordsman. He considers duelling something of a dance, and he is so well controlled that he has never inadvertently injured anyone. The Germans are now imitating our chevalier. Another talented German, Monsieur Mozart, when he returned to Paris six years ago, was startled that the new form of the symphonie concertante had become so prevalent.

Bologne and Mozart are friends of course. Mozart even took to citing his music, such as the presto of his own Symphonie Concertante in E-flat Major, where it echoes a passage from the rondo in Bologne's Violin Concert in A Major. But I speak too much and must bore you both."

"Not at all, this is all very interesting," responded George. "I am very fond of Bologne's music. His first sonata was played at the unveiling ceremony of the zebra. I am greatly looking forward to witnessing his own skill this evening—although I understand the music will be more lighthearted."

"That is good to hear, Monsieur du Paon. Other than making the acquaintance of your elegant companion, my reason for approaching you is that we have speculated amongst our members whether you might consider joining our small assembly. It will not be difficult to secure the required support from three members, as your fame now precedes you. One purpose of the Société is to mix people and opinions, and you would be a great addition to our present menagerie," continued d'Orgny, with a characteristic aristocratic affectation in tone. "But I am ambushing you when you merely intended to have a pleasant afternoon with your charming companion. We are playing one of Bologne's romances today. Please consider our invitation at your leisure, and perhaps send me a note when you have had time to consider it, and we may discuss this matter further?" With a grand gesture, d'Orgny turned and headed into the hall, a servant carrying a cello wrapped in a blanket closely behind him.

"Apologies, Jeanne—that was quite a waterfall!"

"No, no, I find all this interesting. I hear many things I had no idea about. So, this Bologne is a chevalier, he wrote the music that we will hear today, he is playing the violin, your comte has an instrument called cello, and you will join him in his loge?" summarised Jeanne.

Laughing good-heartedly, George acknowledged that this was a fair summary of what had been said and gestured towards the queue. Recollections of the blue dress briefly drifted by in his mind, a whiff of his past. "Let's head into the hall, shall we Jeanne?"

"Yes, let's go. Hey, do you see who is ahead of us in line?"

"Not really. Who do you recognise?" replied George in a worried tone. Perhaps she was seeing someone from her time as the princess?

"There, about a dozen people in front of us in the queue, almost by the door, is Inspecteur Lenoir."

"Oh God, let us avoid him. I cannot fathom another one of his lectures at this moment. That is really too much for today. He'll ask us about the pileus, or more probably hold us up pontificating on one random subject or another. Please don't catch his eye."

"Not so easy, he must have eyes at the back of his head," exclaimed Jeanne, breaking the tension that George felt about the outing with her.

The queue had shortened as many people had already taken their places during the discussion with d'Orgny. George was briefly disoriented as his eyes grew accustomed to the darkness of the hallway—and Jeanne gripped his arm a bit more snugly—but soon they could see the shimmering light from the candles in the concert hall. George showed proof of his subscription, and they were led by a young woman to their seats. Discreetly handing her a few coins, George invited Jeanne to take the place to his right, a distinction he suspected might be lost on her.

The orchestra was already seated and consisted of fifteen musicians. A row of candles shone on them directly, while a large chandelier added more indirect light. George needlessly pointed out the rather easily identifiable Bologne.

"To his right is, of course, d'Orgny, with his cello," he indicated. "There are really four sizes of these string instruments. Bologne has a violin, and you see two more. Then the bigger one—d'Orgny's—is the cello. To their right you see two big violins—or small celli—these are violas."

"But why all these different sizes? It's like the rabbits we worked on last year. What were they called? Argenté, Bourbonnais, and Harlequin?"

"That's right—that was a rather fun commission." George recalled Gaston's embarrassing howls of laughter as he had put the rabbits in various risqué poses. "The violins are a bit like that, but the smaller they are, the higher pitch they have. Next to the violins there is a harpsichord, the big box with the keyboard, and then several wind instruments. Those are the ones that musicians blow into to generate sounds—the smallest ones are piccolos, then a bassoon, clarinet, and trombone. Like the violins, the bigger the lower, the smaller the higher pitch."

To his surprise, she concluded, "And the whole point is getting the whole to be more than the sum of the instruments—that is music?"

Not exposed to a surprise royal visit, the musicians had mostly resorted to simple afternoon coats, with d'Orgny standing out through the reflections of his rich silk fabric. A sheet in the hallway announced the title of the romance: *Love and Death of the Poor Little Bird.* It opened with the bird celebrating its delight at the return of spring and then quickly transitioned to a slower, more serious part, where he softly announced his love, soulfully and seductively. The music twisted and turned with the sound of birds hopping from branch to branch. When the lovesick bird was rejected, the birds began singing a reproachful song to the cruel object of his affection, who had chosen another. Then, plaintively, the poor abandoned bird died, wrapped in a melancholic melody, yearning for the happy years that had been lost. The piece sputtered to an end as the poor bird died, loveless and falling from his branch.

As they shuffled out together with the crowd, George held Jeanne's elbow with some emphasis. Having traversed the dark corridor in silence, they emerged into the afternoon light of the courtyard.

"I am going to America," Jeanne blurted out. With no reaction from George, she continued, "In France, I seem destined to always dress as another."

Collecting himself, and still blinking in the bright sunlight, which suddenly felt much more offensive, George responded, "But Jeanne, most of life is playing roles. You saw the comte play a Freemason Grand Master and also be a musician. Your and my roles with each other might also be different, who knows."

By the blank look on her face, George knew she was not hearing him. Lost in her conviction and seemingly not registering his words, Jeanne affirmed that she had made up her mind.

A group of jugglers and fire spewers presently overtook them, their sounds and merriness drowning out any remnants of their conversation.

12

The Part and the Whole

As George and Nicolas settled at their usual table in the Café de Foy, George's attention was drawn to a young woman holding court at a table across the room. The light from an adjacent window spilled across her arrestive features.

"Have you ever enjoyed the experience of meeting Germaine de Staël?" enquired Nicolas.

"I'm afraid not," George answered. "But her new husband was at the zebra presentation, as you will recall."

"She's quite the hurricane. Precocious, outspoken . . . and she has a sharp wit."

One was immediately struck by her piercing gaze—with pupils perhaps further dilated by an affection for laudanum. Radiant eyes compensated for a slightly plump face. Her dress included a highly unusual and rather unfashionable green turban struggling to constrain an avalanche of black curls, competing with a particularly revealing décolleté, even by the standards of the Palais-Royal. She appeared to exude a manic energy, and that singular capacity some individuals inhabit to go from one genuinely lived emotion or reasoning to another in the shortest space of time—leaving the exhausted observers reeling at her dexterity of heart and mind.

George recalled past conversations as his friend had described the extraordinary girl that he had come across in various salon evenings, the daughter of the minister Nicolas knew well. Born as the daughter of the immensely wealthy Genevan banker, Necker, and raised in Paris, where her father ultimately became the finance minister of Louis XVI, Germaine Necker worshipped her father. At the same time, she resembled much more her mother, Suzanne Curchod, whom she accordingly despised. The mother was an idiosyncratically brilliant woman, hosting one of Paris's most luminous salons, albeit with a necrophiliac bent. She requested to be embalmed and would describe in detail her desire to float in a bath of alcohol for many centuries in a crypt at the family château at Coppet. Upon hearing of her talents and unorthodox opinions from Nicolas, George could well imagine Germaine having her own glittering salon someday, where she would hold the pen on the early drafts of the increasingly revolutionary texts that were circulating and become a lightning rod for some of the leading Enlightenment intellectuals of the day. Both Curchod and Necker came from protestant Genevan pastors' families. Suzanne had received a truly Renaissance-like education and was well versed in Latin, Greek, mathematics, and philosophy, and ably played two instruments—but she had no money. Almost marrying Gibbon, who remained a faithful friend for life, she hunted for a rich man. Necker was one of the wealthiest men in Europe, and truly loved her—at least at the beginning of their marriage, and after her death.

Not trusting any governess, her mother had raised and educated her daughter in home isolation until the age of twelve, when she finally selected a playmate for her. This was the first time Germaine had interacted with another child or had a friend of a similar age. Until then, Germaine's childhood conversations had been with family friends such as Rousseau, Voltaire, or d'Alembert—great for the intellect, but hardly serving the emotional development of a young girl. Father, mother, and daughter all wrote furiously, often sending multiple letters to each other in the course of an evening, from one room to the next. The family was very rich—and very odd.

Although Palais-Royal rumours had it that she really had aspired to be her father's lover, Germaine opted to marry the Swedish Baron de Staël, whom George had met at the unveiling of the zebra. Thus, earlier in the year, at the age of twenty-two, Germaine had wed the consciously unsuspecting Baron Eric Magnus Staël von Holstein, secretary of the Swedish embassy in Paris. The baron's bride was rich and endowed with a thoroughly warped view of the world, and a mind fed almost exclusively on the drawing room debates between the intellectuals of the day. While Germaine was never described as beautiful in a conventional sense, above all else, she was irresistibly charismatic. Many men were fascinated by her, and George imagined that she required the fascination of many—both serially and simultaneously—to hold her considerable interest.[51]

As she chaired her table, Germaine was the recently minted author of her first book.[52] *Sophie or the Secret Sentiments* was a cathartic and poorly written novel, but it did the job of liberating her from desiring her father. It was a suitably and barely veiled autobiographical work, shocking her mother when she unabashedly read it to her parents—or at least rumour had it. But the therapy worked, and she was now free to turn to other lovers. Her free and independent attitude, and her intellectual superiority, upended many conventions. This made her the darling of some, but she incurred the hatred of many others, although she would always be generous and faithful to friends for life.

"Two years ago, Kant asked, 'What is Enlightenment?' And offered 'dare to understand' as a response." George could overhear de Staël taunting her company.

"Who is this Kant?" a man in a green silk redingote shouted across the table.

"Forgive Noailles's ignorance, as he does not read German," she said to general laughter. "A philosopher from across the Rhine, with a deserved reputation," she went on to explain.

---

51 Later, Napoleon thought her one of his greatest threats, commissioning a daily briefing on her whereabouts and specifying the distance at which she should physically remain from him at all times.

52 Although written in 1786, it was not published until 1790.

"The Enlightenment may be French at heart, but its brain spreads beyond our borders to Germany and Scotland."

A lady whose black dress suggested either a state of mourning or an excessive inclination towards religious modesty responded, "Herr Kant subscribes to the quintessentially German idea that our individual perception is at the core of understanding the world. He is unconvinced by the views that some of us hold dear, that it is human reason in which we express our unique, God-given nature. And it is logical reasoning that allows us to overcome our conflicts and resolve our differences."

Noailles in the green coat grumbled something to the extent that his intuition was also God-given, entirely French, and had served him well to successfully command the king's troops in battle with the same Germans.

Effortlessly remaining the focal point of the conversation, wildly gesturing, Germaine retorted, "Escorting poor souls to their death in a tacit partnership with the generals on the other side is hardly a celebration of the value of intuition. Our friend Rousseau wants to make a religion of reason, which in turn contains the roots of its destruction."

"Ironically, Descartes put the individual at the heart of his philosophy with his 'cogito, ergo sum,'" Noailles stated, "but for Descartes, it was the rational-thinking individual. Rousseau picked up the baton, but centred his philosophy on the sensing individual, grounding knowledge in experience. But life is not merely the cross section of one's experiences, as with the empiricists—it forms the centre of the self as the basis for human development."

Germaine raised a hand in exclamation and held the attention of the table while she took a sip from the glass that had just been refilled. Satisfied at the silence extracted, she responded, "As is the case with any religion, inevitably someone will claim the higher ground and not surrender it until blood is shed. Kant attempts to accommodate reality by pointing out the limits of reason. While that is philosophically appealing, I wonder whether it is politically prudent. Opening this door has the danger of taking us back into a world where human passion is the basis for justifying the heroic action that an individual desires. We can use reason to conclude a path forward that we share—and then use emotions to drum up support from others less so inclined."

"For someone educated by Voltaire, you have a surprising optimism about the capacity of people to listen to each other," intervened a man to Germaine's left, adding maliciously, "Kant is said to have had a portrait of Rousseau on the wall of his study."

"Well, Voltaire mainly visited us when his supply of coffee was low. His interest in convincing a Swiss child of his views was rather limited, as precocious as she might have appeared to him." Thus Germaine sidestepped the diversion and pursued the course. "To consistently apply reason, we must assume that the world is built from discrete elements, each independent of each other. Only then can we reason deductively about them. Kant suggests that this would be approximately right, but in principle wrong. So, to save our deductive capacity of reasoning, we have no choice but to overlook it, on occasion."

Noailles cut through the conversation: "What does our rich culture have to learn from Germans or the British for that matter? The British are so dependent on French skill and innovation that they send their zebras to be stuffed in Paris and even steal our melodies for their national anthem. The Marquise de Créquy tells the story of how Lully wrote a song to distract Louis XIV when they painfully removed an anal fistula. Händel later heard the tune and used it to write the anthem that the British chose as their own."

He softly sang:

"Dear God, save the King!
Dear God, save the King!
Long live the King!
The ever glorious,
Louis Victorious,
Sees his enemies,
Ever subdued,
Dear God . . ."[53]

A group of men loudly entered the Café de Foy, and the ever-gracious Mathilde led them to a table. Their rowdy boasts of self-described exploits in one of the adjacent houses of pleasure of the Palais-Royal drowned out the conversations, as well as Lully's motet at the Necker table.

Straightening himself on his chair, easily swivelling through the low friction between the embossed leather covering of the

---

53 Grand Dieu, sauvez le Roi! Grand Dieu, vengez le Roi! Vive le Roi! Qu'à jamais glorieux, Louis victorieux Voye ses ennemis Toujours soumis! Grand Dieu, sauvez le Roi! Grand Dieu, vengez le Roi! Vive le Roi! Source: Créquy, 1839.

seat and the silk of his breeches, Nicolas turned his attention back to George. "It is the Law of History. It is up to politics to deliver the kind of society where man can fully express his reason. And it is up to science to cultivate that reason. In such a society, man is free. And that freedom necessarily extends to women; to Protestants, Jews, and Muslims; to the poor; and to negroes. Privilege is only insufferable if it is not based on the respect of the human rights of others. And since it most often is based in despotism or the reign of sheer habit, it does not respect reason."

"That is admirable, *mon cher*," rebutted George, "but you first assume that all men will act reasonably, and secondly that even if they did, that the whole would be reasonable. It may not."

"How could it not be? If the parts are reasonable, so is the whole."

"Could there be something added in the whole? The landscape around your charming house in Mantes, where the Seine flows peacefully under the gaze of the willows, where the hen cries its heart out, and butterflies dwell on the petals of wild roses. And yet will you not concede that nature is more than the sum of the river, the fauna, and the flora? Do we not experience a unity of nature that transcends its parts? And what is in harmony could also be in dissonance. Could the collective reasonableness not unleash a fury, no longer tamed by the will of an imperfect sovereign?"

"But this unity of nature is a mere emotion, which must be submitted to the light of reason."

"Very well. Let's shine reason on the queen's zebra. I have taken it apart; I can see its skin, hooves, and tail each lying on a separate table. *Cher* marquis, perpetual secretary of the Academy of Sciences, can your reason reassemble a zebra—or do you, perhaps, find there are parts missing?"

"True enough," grumbled Condorcet. "So are the missing pieces God's works? Must we resign our ambition to understand the world on our terms and assign a final place to revealed truths? Surely, we can leave open the question and trust that future exploration will deliver a satisfactory explanation? Perhaps we should follow Spallanzani's suggestion that we name occult the bits that fit between the whole and the parts. An occult that leads the whole to emerge from the parts?"

"That is a valid suggestion, but it is not a mere missing part of a puzzle; this casts doubt on the very idea that there is a puzzle for which the pieces can be gradually found."

Mathilde had directed one of the servants to refill their coupes and briefly stopped by their table. "I hope the debate across the room is not drowning out your own learned reflections, gentlemen," she said graciously. "Mademoiselle Necker's company can be quite loud."

"Our gratitude for taking such good care of us, Mathilde," said Nicolas, tipping his hand towards the glasses. "The fascinating company you attract is certainly a defining feature of your establishment. And it is the very mixing of perspectives that leads to the best new thoughts, especially when fuelled by your excellent champagne!"

Such fleeting conversations provided Mathilde with an excuse to invite George, with a short blink of her eyes, to linger at the end of the evening.

Changing the subject once Mathilde had left them alone, Nicolas enquired after Jeanne, not having had news since he had returned her to George's workshop after the evening at Madame Helvétius's. His voice betrayed a twinge of guilt in having used her for a social experiment. Yet with some malicious gratification, Nicolas commented, "The multiple enquiries I have received for introductions to the princess from disoriented potential suitors surprised me. They all complained that they failed to pinpoint her in the geography of the Parisian salons."

Momentarily frowning and grasping his chin, he continued. "On the return journey, Jeanne was taciturn, only enquiring as to when she might return the clothes—having handed me the necklace as soon as the fiacre's door had closed. Her face did not betray a thought or emotion when I then gently informed her that the clothes were hers to own. I had—wrongly, apparently—assumed that she would assume they were. Or rather, I hadn't even considered that she would ask to return them. In any case, they are hers to keep."

"A perfectly incongruous possession for a woman in her position, but generous of you. I will need to replace her . . . as she is leaving the workshop next August," flatlined George. He described how after the Saint-Georges performance, Jeanne had announced she would leave for America. "After your outing, Jeanne had been all excited about her discussion with the American ambassador—or probably by the respect and attention Jefferson paid her. I suppose he gave her an image of how she might be seen and treated in America. It's possible, it's possible—but she also could be in for one of those Russian mountain rides."[54] Reflecting on that afternoon, he had been lightly hurt that she did not prelude or preclude this with an appreciation of all that he had done for her. Though he realised that social assent often required leaving behind bridges that were no longer useful, he had hoped for something more meaningful with Jeanne.

"Have you been able to find some peace with Violette's memory?"

George was startled by Nicolas's question. He stared intently at his glass.

"Jeanne sometimes provided a distant echo of her—so I can well imagine it might awaken dried tears," Nicolas continued. "When I—or should I say we—spent the evening with her as Princess de Savoie, I was struck by the occasional parallel, a shake of the head or the lift of an eyebrow."

"Thank you, Nicolas," George replied, looking up to his friend, and they settled together into sentient silence.

George had indeed felt a twinge of sorrow, as Jeanne had been a link to his sister, oddly similar in a few ways, although the two had never met. But he realised perfectly well that those

54 In Russia beginning in the seventeenth century, they used sleds to slide down hills constructed from ice. This was the precursor to the roller coaster, and they were known in Europe as Russian mountains. Ironically, the modern Russian translation of roller coaster is American mountain.

links were nothing but an illusion that human minds construct to evade emptiness. Nicolas's delicacy touched him, as it was not always part of the rituals of their friendship, which retained a hint of formality, perhaps due to the chasm in their societal ranks.

"And what does she plan to do with herself once she crosses the ocean? Is there a plan of some sort in place?"

George explained to Nicolas that he had offered her a generous parting payment to help her set up a new life. "It was the least I could do," George added, not mentioning what was perhaps a touch of jealousy when Jeanne had described how Thomas Jefferson had promised he would provide introductions to his circles in Boston, offering her services as a portraitist of pets and heirs. Boldly, she had then hinted to Jefferson that her family was impoverished, notwithstanding the appearance of nobility. George assumed that Jefferson had suspected that she may not have been entirely what she pretended to be, but he was enough of a judge of character to be impressed by her quiet perseverance.

"Jeanne also told me something about a young slave girl whom Jefferson's relatives had just shipped to France, at his request. He was being pressured by his compatriots to send her back, and was considering having Jeanne accompany the girl home. It had struck Jeanne that Jefferson seemed to care a lot about the girl. Perhaps about Jeanne, too, it seems. Anyway, I suppose if it helps her become a painter . . ."[55]

---

55 Sally Hemings, with whom Jefferson was to have several children, actually arrived in Paris a year later, in 1787, aged fourteen. Abigail Adams had unsuccessfully pressured Jefferson to send her back to America.

"Jeanne an American painter!" exclaimed Nicolas, tactfully ignoring the salacious anecdote on the American ambassador, as well as sidestepping George's bruised feelings. "But losing her is an unfortunate consequence of our little experiment. She will do well less shackled by the social convention required on our shores. Jefferson enthralled her with his stories from Lahontan's writing, and I just hope she does not have too great of an expectation of the state of equality and freedom. Their indigenous culture may well have had a greater influence on French Enlightenment philosophers than it has locally in the Americas."

"Yes, a great step for Enlightenment. Her departure is hopefully a gain for American art, and for Jeanne herself, but it is a loss for my own small world," concluded George.

13

Adrift

In the last few hectic weeks, Jeanne had insisted on completing the work on the platypus. George had been able to find a set of drawings from the royal library, although many seemed to have been mostly drawn from the imagination of the artist, bearing scant resemblance to the limp skin that lay prepared in the workshop waiting to be resurrected through wire and straw. They struggled with nature seemingly just expressing oddness. Why? What might the emergence of this amalgamation of other animal parts express? Should it waddle like a duck or crawl like a lizard? An unease had settled between the taxidermist and his assistant after their evening at the concert. George could not help but think that the resulting work was merely conventional. Jeanne had silently concurred.

The day of Jeanne's departure had come. George and Gaston walked her to the embarkment on the Seine. A river boat would take her to Le Havre, where the trans-Atlantic seafaring ships departed for Boston. Gaston carried her bag, which contained the few possessions she had, notably the green dress from her evening as the Princess de Savoie. Nicolas had been kind enough to donate generous funds, supplementing those George had provided. Ambassador Jefferson had arranged for her to stay with Bostonian acquaintances to introduce Jeanne into her new world. Gaston whistled as they walked the otherwise silent and short distance to the river port. Whether it was to distract himself or George, or both of them, George didn't know.

"There is your ship. The *Hirondelle*, isn't it?" offered George to break the awkwardness.

"Indeed. That is the one. I am certain it is indeed my ship."

After a few short words and embraces from the two men, Jeanne was on the plank waving back in time, before fading into the crowd assembled on the deck. With a grim nod to George, Gaston walked away with a perceptible slump in his shoulders.

George had agreed to meet Nicolas to distract himself—perhaps it would achieve more than Gaston's whistling, though George was not hopeful.

Leaving the royal statue on his left, George entered the Tuileries gardens from the place Louis XV. An invigorating headwind blew from the Louvre over the Tuileries palace. Autumn leaves twirled over the gravel-covered pathways lined with chestnut trees. He had wanted to reflect on the details of the past weeks' events to his friend and remove himself from Jeanne's departure. Nicolas had only picked up fragments of the zebra's story from conversations in various salons.

Like George, Nicolas also wore a plain sturdy woollen cape and boots to dispel the cold, a welcome visual reprieve in the habitual swirl of colour, ribbons, heels, and feathers. The wind caught and blew away George's hat; he ran after it and found it as it had come to rest against a broad tree trunk. As he was bending to pick up his hat, George noticed his right knee cracking slightly more loudly than he had grown accustomed to. He made a note to be more diligent about exercising in the morning. Returning to Nicolas and catching his breath while pointing at the straight line of trees, George observed, "We hunker after regularity. Where it is questionable, we simply create it. Our doctors inspect our excrements and declare seeing patterns with conviction."

"Regularities doubtlessly exist. Newton could predict the passage of stellar objects with astounding precision. On the other hand, the pattern of a zebra's stripes appears to have no rhyme or reason; they are all different, yet recognisable as a zebra," rebutted Nicolas. "After all, Pascal once observed that he 'held it impossible to know the parts without knowing the whole, and likewise impossible to know the whole without knowing the parts individually.'" Acknowledging the thought with a short hum, the two men walked in silence.

"And Jeanne?" enquired Nicolas.

"She sailed this morning."

Nicolas grunted silently and after a long pause, gently steered the conversation back to the zebra's wake.

The disgrace of one of their peers had struck a chord with the aristocracy. It had the predictable effect of triggering memories of new events that demonstrated their long-standing distance from Beaubourg. George narrated the circumstances of the theft, the journey to Ville d'Avray, Lenoir's lectures on logic, airships, pileus, and man's relation to the world, the anticlimactic return of the zebra to Paris, the visit of the British envoy with the platypus, and the departure of the crate for London.

"The travels and travails of a stuffed animal," exclaimed Nicolas after taking in all the twists and turns of the zebra's recovery. "So did Beaubourg's red boxes unlock the secret to the platypus's constitution?"

"No. Or not really. The mind's journey was highly eventful and very memorable, but not useful in any utilitarian sense. Quite a disappointment after the perspective Lenoir had painted. Jeanne had great expectations but said she had mostly bathed in colours and patterns."

"Interesting, but not entirely surprising." Nicolas glanced furtively at George. "As most things, pileus travel takes some practice for one to head to the desired destination. Perhaps try once more? Still, the recovery of the zebra is quite a tale. Any news on Beaubourg?"

"He was released from the Bastille following the intervention of some of his friends who were fearful of a precedent. He was then exiled to remain at least a thousand miles from Paris. I suppose he will neither settle in England nor in Saxony, where he would hardly be welcomed, but that leaves plenty of other options. Two of his men were executed and the others given a hundred lashes. He must have been disappointed that his own punishment had not been consistent with his views on justice: retribution above proportionality."

"It is likely he actually intended this kind of justice for others, not for himself," murmured Nicolas. "And any insights on how the Queen of England appreciated your zebra?"

"The ship carrying it across the Manche was lost in a sudden storm. The zebra probably did not sink, as its wooden crate was on the deck and diligently sealed with wax, so it may reappear on a distant shore."

"Perhaps on an African coast?"

"That would be fitting."

"It has been a wild year. But I fear this is not the last storm that we have failed to deduce."

Postscript

The stage, the décor, and many of the characters in this story are broadly historical, drawing on stories and facts of the time. Many of these stories and facts come from the literature listed in the Bibliography and Additional Literature. On a few occasions I have taken some liberty with the dates to fit our narrative.

George du Paon and Jeanne Laplume are entirely fictional and so are the dialogues. The Marquis Nicolas de Condorcet is a major historical figure who perished on the way to the guillotine in 1794 as did so many of his age, such as Madame du Barry. Germaine de Staël was a sometimes-underrated giant of the period, who sidestepped the bloody fury through a Swiss exile to lead a colourful life, including remaining a recurring nightmare for Napoleon.

The historic backdrop serves merely to explore the curious conjunction at a historical crossroad of Reductionism and the

Enlightenment, a connection that was to yield both great benefit and great damage in the centuries to come, as it cemented man's separation from nature. It was also an opportunity to simply spin a tale.

Some have observed that in the nineteenth century, Lord Rothschild drove a cart pulled by three zebras and a horse to Buckingham palace, and other images even show people riding zebras, contradicting the eighteenth-century conclusion that zebras are untameable. They are: in principle as a species, and evolutionary biologists now understand why. But as with everything in nature, there are exceptions, such as the few tamed individuals on record.

It seems that the emancipation of human thought from divine guidance in the eighteenth century that was coined as the Enlightenment spuriously crossed paths with the state of science of the day, in particular mechanical science—or more precisely kinetics—to cement Reductionism as the method of choice for the newly discovered rational thought.

Like George in this book, many thinkers and writers in the following centuries expressed their reserves about this marriage of ideas. Replacing the complexity of the natural and social world with concepts applicable to pullies and with statistics from rolling dice seems opportunistic at best. The arc of this history of thought is far from linear and perhaps it is not even an arc. While Madame de Staël, with considerable foresight, expressed her worries that German subjectivism might someday lead to a catastrophic regime, rationalist France much earlier succumbed to Jacobin terror and was followed by

Napoleonic megalomania, not the reasoned and balanced governance foreseen by the Enlightenment philosophers.

The Romantic tradition of the early nineteenth century rejected Reductionism, but it still ruled in many of the scientific disciplines. Some of the social sciences were engulfed in the early twentieth century, particularly economics, becoming ensnarled through the temptations of the easy mathematics of closed equilibrium systems. Still, cracks continued to appear. In the ivory tower of mathematics, Euler's project to base all of algebra completely on a small, finite set of axioms capsized when Bertrand Russell pointed out a fatal flaw, with Gödel adding the proverbial final straw that showed that the project was impossible. Mathematics would never provide a perfect model of reality. In physics, Schrödinger's incompleteness theorem—better known as a cat story—evidenced more cracks. The humanities retained a broader frame, sidestepping fundamentalist attempts such as in Wittgenstein's *Tractatus*. The humanities, the arts, and personal experience continued to nag us about the gap between the intuited reality and the Reductionist training we had received, making room for what Spallanzani cited as the "occult," where the whole is more than the sum of the parts.

Today we know that order in complex systems emerges through random stochastic interactions that provide the fodder for organising principles to pick out and coalesce winners. So it was for the emergence of the ideas of the Enlightenment themselves. It is perhaps no coincidence that the art of the time escalated from baroque to rococo, with its twirling interacting shapes and ornaments that ultimately blend into a collective image. It takes stories, sidesteps, and ornaments to craft the space of an idea—and so it is with *Falling in Love While Stuffing a Zebra* in which the side-alleys are the fodder of the emergent narrative.

It was not until the 1980s that a concerted effort started to develop a science of complex systems. This holds out the hope that Enlightenment thinking may yet evolve to embrace complexity instead of mechanics—or kinetics!—as a foundational frame.

Fumbling les Lumières would be a tragedy and start a slide down to a much darker age. Enriching it would be a boon to society. Paradoxically, the very core of the Enlightenment is under threat most visibly in the only major country whose governing institutions were designed strictly along its principles.

Still, a scientific occult is a development worth watching.

Bibliography

Adams, William Howard. *The Paris Years of Thomas Jefferson*. Yale University Press, 2000.

Babeau, Albert. *Le Louvre et son histoire*. Firmin-Didot & Cie, Paris, 1895.

Blakemore, Erin. "The Revolutionary War Hero Who Was Openly Gay." History. Updated June 25, 2024. https://www.history.com/news/openly-gay-revolutionary-war-hero-friedrich-von-steuben.

Canales, Jimena. *Bedeviled: A Shadow History of Demons in Science*. Princeton University Press, 2020.

Créquy. *Souvenirs de la Marquise de Créquy de 1710 à 1803*. Garnier Frères, Paris, 1839. http://penelope.uchicago.edu/crequy/chap104.html.

Delille, Jacques. "Dans ce Jardin on ne rencontre."

Dijksterhuis, Eduard J. *De mechanisering van het wereldbeeld*. Meulenhoff, Amsterdam, 1950.

Dumas, Alexandre. *Le Collier de la Reine*. Michel Lévy Frères, Paris, 1860.

Farrell, Molly. "Ben Franklin Put an Abortion Recipe in His Math Textbook." Slate. May 5, 2022. https://slate.com/news-and-politics/2022/05/ben-franklin-american-instructor-textbook-abortion-recipe.html.

Gervais, Charles-Hubert, and Joseph de Lafonds. *Hypermnestre, Libretto.* s.n., S.l, monographic. 1716. https://lccn.loc.gov/2011564269.

Haslip, Joan. *Madame du Barry: The Wages of Beauty*. Grove Weidenfeld, New York, 1992.

Herold, Christopher. *Mistress to an Age: A life of Madame de Staël*. Grove Press, New York, 1958.

Jefferson, Thomas. "From Thomas Jefferson to Buffon, 1 October 1787." *Founders Online*. National Archives. https://founders.archives.gov/documents/Jefferson/01-12-02-0191.

Journal de Paris. September 5, 1786. https://gallica.bnf.fr/ark:/12148/bpt6k1055275h.item.

Meghji, Shafik. "London's Centre of Intrigue and Scandal." BBC. May 10, 2021. https://www.bbc.com/travel/article/20210509-londons-centre-of-intrigue-and-scandal.

Nature. "History of the Public Lighting of Paris." *Nature* 132, 888–889. 1933.

Panzanelli, Roberta, and Preti-Hamard, Monica (ed.). *La circulation des œuvres d'art, 1789-1848*. Presses universitaires de Rennes, 2007.

Prioleau, Betsy. *Seductress: Women Who Ravished the World and Their Lost Art of Love*. Penguin, New York, 2003.

Thiney, Jack. *Mort ou Vif–Chronique d'une taxidermie comtemporaine*. Editions de La Martiniere, Paris, 2014.

Vergé-Franceschi, Michel, and Anna Moretti. *Une Histoire Érotique de Versailles.* Editions Payot & Rivages, Paris, 2015.

Welten, Joost. *De Vergeten Prinsessen van Thorn (1700-1794).* Sterck de Vreese, Gorredijk, 2019.

Wikipedia. "Platypus." Accessed November 12, 2024. https://en.wikipedia.org/wiki/Platypus.

Wikipedia. "Tuileries Garden." Accessed February 17, 2024. https://en.wikipedia.org/wiki/Tuileries_Garden.

Additional Literature

Alberti, Samuel J. M. M., ed. *The Afterlives of Animals—A Museum Menagerie*. University of Virginia Press, 2011.

Antonetti, Guy. *Louis Phillippe*. Fayard, Paris, 1994.

Badinter, Elisabeth, and Robert Badinter. *Condorcet–Un intellectuel en politique*. Fayard, Paris, 1989.

Banat, Gabriel. "Le Chevalier de Saint-Georges, Man of Music and Gentleman-at-Arms: The Life and Times of an Eighteenth-Century Prodigy." *Black Music Research Journal* 10, no. 2 (1990): 177–212.

Beccaria, Cesare Bonesana di. *An Essay on Crimes and Punishments*. 1764.

Buffon, Georges-Louis Leclerc Comte de. *Histoire naturelle*. 36 volumes. Online edition, http://www.buffon.cnrs.fr.

Delseny, Michel. "L'Académie des sciences: 350 ans d'existence." *Revue de l'AMOPA*, no. 214 (2017): 13–17.

Denys, Catherine, Brigitte Marin, and Vincent Milliot. *Réformer la police–Les memoires policiers en Europe au XVIIIème siècle.* Presses Universitaires de France, Paris, 2009.

Doorman, Maarten. *Rousseau en ik: over de erfzonde van de authenticiteit*. Bakker, Amsterdam, 2012.

Dupouy, Alexandre et Romain. *Guide pratique fidèle et illustré des filles de joie du Palais-Royal.* Hyppolyte, Editions Astarté, Paris, 1999.

Fletcher, Michael-Shawn et al. "Indigenous Knowledge and the Shackles of Wilderness." *Proceedings of the National Academy of Sciences* 118, no. 40 (2021): e2022218118.

Foster, Charles. *Being a Beast: Adventures Across the Species Divide.* Picador, London, 2017.

Gottlieb, Anthony. *The Dream of Enlightenment: The Rise of Modern Philosophy.* Liveright, New York, 2017.

Graeber, David, and David Wengrow. *The Dawn of Everything–A New History of Humanity.* Allen Lane, London, 2021.

Kale, Steven. *French Salons–High Society and Political Sociability from the Old Regime to the Revolution of 1848.* John Hopkins University Press, Baltimore, 2006.

De Lom d'Arce La Hontan, Louis Armand. *Dialogues de M. le baron de Lahontan et d'un sauvage dans l'Amerique*. Veuve Boeteman, Amsterdam, 1704.

Pearl, Judea, and Dana Mackenzie. *The Book of Why–The New Science of Cause and Effect.*

Pinker, Steve. *Enlightenment Now–The Case for Reason, Science, Humanism and Progress.* Penguin, London, 2018.

Plumb, Christopher. *Exotic Animals in Eighteenth-Century Britain*. A thesis submitted to The University of Manchester for the degree of PhD in Museology in the Faculty of Humanities. 2010.

De Quesnay, Francois. *Le despotisme de la Chine.* 1767. http://courses.umass.edu/pols294p/documents.html/quesnay.pdf.

Quoy-Bodin, Jean-Luc. "L'orchestre de La Société Olympique En 1786." *Revue de Musicologie* 70, no. 1 (1984): 95–107.

Roberts, William. *Memorials of Christie's–A record of art sales from 1766 to 1896.* George Bell and Sons, London, 1897.

Trouilleux, Rodolphe. *Le Palais-Royal–Un demi-siècle de folies 1780-1830.* Bernard Giovanangeli Éditeur, Paris, 2010.

De Waresquiel, Emmanuel. *Talleyrand, Le Prince Immobile.* Fayard, Paris, 2006.

Wood, Gordon. *The Americanization of Benjamin Franklin.* Penguin Press, London, 2001.

Wulf, Andrea. *The Invention of Nature: The Adventures of Alexander von Humboldt, the Lost Hero of Science.* John Murray, London, 2015.

Zhou, Yang et al. "Platypus and Echidna Genomes Reveal Mammalian Biology and Evolution." *Nature* 592 (2021): 756–762.

About the Author

DR. ROLAND KUPERS is an author and an advisor on Complexity, Resilience, and Energy Transition. He is the Lead Architect of UNEP's International Methane Emissions Observatory, and a Professor of Practice at Arizona State University.

A theoretical physicist by training, Roland spent a decade each at AT&T and at Shell in various senior executive functions, including group head for Sustainable Development and Vice President Global LNG. He has a long-running interest in complexity theory and its impacts. This novel is a whimsical exploration of the historical context when we fumbled complexity.

He has published widely, including in *Harvard Business Review*, on Project Syndicate, etc. His books include *Hester van Eeghen—A World of Bags* (nai010 2024) and *A Climate Policy Revolution: What the Science of Complexity Reveals about Saving the Planet* (Harvard University Press 2020). He has coauthored *Complexity and the Art of Public Policy: Solving Society's Problems from the Bottom Up* (Princeton University Press 2014), *The*

Essence of Scenarios (Amsterdam University Press 2014), and *Turbulence: A Corporate Framing of Resilience* (Amsterdam University Press 2014).

In 2010, Roland was a coauthor of a report commissioned by the German government on a New Growth Path for Europe, applying a complexity lens to climate economics. He has been an advisor to the Environmental Defense Fund, the World Resources Institute, and the Rockefeller Foundation.

Roland is a Dutch national; his travels have made him fluent in five languages.